# Call Me Katherine

## a Novel

### Virginia Woods Meyer

*Virginia Meyer*

## Dedication

For my family

# Call Me Katherine

### a Novel

## Virginia Woods Meyer

NorLightsPress.com
2721 Tulip Tree Rd.
Nashville, IN 47448

Printed in the United States of America
ISBN: 978-1-935254-15-7

Book and Cover Design by Nadene Carter
Poem: Used by permission, Mary Mac, 1-800-Life-101

First printing, 2009

# Acknowledgements

When I decided to retire, the question most frequently asked was, "What will you do, now?" I had four ready answers: spend more time with family and friends, travel some, exercise more, and write.

Participation in the Senior Writers' Workshop offered through the Institute for Extended Learning and the Community Colleges of Spokane has provided an outlet for fulfilling that dream. Through this program I have acquired technical skills. In addition, the classes have been a source of motivation and encouragement, while introducing me to a wide array of people with whom I have formed friendships that enrich my life.

I am especially appreciative of the support of fellow writer Pam Albee whose careful reading of this manuscript and resulting comments have helped bring this story and its characters to life. Another classmate, Chuck Lyons generously shared his knowledge of computers and steered me to his editor, Nadene Carter of NorlightsPress at a time when this book had been consigned to oblivion in my desk drawer. Nadene's kind and considerate guidance through the editing and publication process has been a delightful experience.

When approaching a project such as this, every writer needs a sounding board to verify that the words written hold meaning for others, so to all the friends who read this work and assured me it was worth pursuing, thank you.

Acknowledgment is also offered to Mary Mac, who generously granted posthumous permission to use a love

poem written by her father, Peter McWilliams—a poem
I remembered from the time it was first published many
years ago.

Virginia Woods Meyer

# Chapter 1

*H*er day's work completed, Kitty tidied her desk. Friday night—a whole two days to enjoy these glorious late spring days. Her thoughts returned to the moment and she jotted a to-do list for the next week. No dallying around for her; she'd be ready to go to work the moment she arrived on Monday morning.

Clutter obliterated, she closed the last desk drawer. The intercom buzzed.

"Kitty, will you please stop by my office before you leave. There's something I'd like to discuss with you." Her boss's voice—casual, matter of fact as usual.

"Sure, Ed. I'm just winding things up. I'll be right there."

With a final glance about the cubicle to be sure all was in order, Kitty lifted her jacket from the hook by the door, took her purse from the bottom desk drawer, touched up her lipstick and proceeded down the hall to Ed's office. Her thoughts shifted to plans for the night's dinner—enough meatloaf left from last night. She'd pop a couple of potatoes in the microwave, steam some carrots with a little mint the way Phil liked them, and toss a salad. Plenty of time for that even if the boss kept her a little late. Bringing this train of thought to an end, she knocked on Ed's door and entered.

"Thanks for stopping, Kitty." Turning in his chair to face her, Ed launched directly into the purpose of this visit. "Remember the special lifestyle series you proposed a few months ago? My mind keeps returning to the possibilities that idea has to offer. The theme fits well with the interests and goals of our *Maine Scene* publication. It's a timely topic and, if done well, could serve as a means to draw an ever-widening element of readers to your *Family Matters* section. Times are changing. I'd like to introduce the series as a regular feature in the new year and want you to take on the project. It will call for a significant time commitment on your part, and of course you'll be compensated accordingly. Are you interested?"

* * * *

Weaving through traffic as she drove the familiar miles from office to home, Kitty fairly bounced with excitement. This was the opportunity she'd hoped and waited for. The idea for the series had come to her even before she landed the job with the magazine five years ago. She loved people and houses, was fascinated with the ways different families lived and intrigued by their dreams and hopes for what they would choose, *if only wishes were horses,* as her grandfather used to say. And now, one of her dreams was about to come true. Tonight she and Phil would celebrate, if only... Please God let him be in a good mood, she thought. She knew he'd be happy for her, but lately he'd seemed so frustrated, depressed by his own situation at the university.

Shifting lanes through traffic she pulled into the entrance of the neighborhood market. There'd be no leftover meatloaf tonight. Tonight would be special—champagne time. They'd enjoy a glass of bubbly and toast her new assignment.

Forty minutes later, having donned a stylish chef's apron to cover her business attire, Kitty efficiently assembled dinner. Four medallion lamb chops lay on a pan ready to pop under the broiler at the last minute. A quick casserole of Romanoff potatoes, rich with the aroma of sour cream, cheese and onion wafted in the air as it baked in the oven. The fresh asparagus, for which she'd spent a small fortune, stood ready and waiting to be steamed. The blender whirred as she whipped together her own blend of herbs and spice for the simple oil and vinegar dressing Phil preferred for his green salad. Knife in hand, she diced and sliced the mix of tomatoes, onions and avocado to toss with the greens. The dishwasher they'd forgotten to turn on last night roared in the background. Engrossed in her preparations, she was totally unaware that Phil had entered the room until he grasped her around the waist, lifted her in the air and began to whirl around the floor of their big farmhouse style kitchen. Playfully he nipped her ear with a kiss as he set her back on her feet, and grinning from ear to ear exclaimed, "Guess what!" Then without waiting for a response announced, "I quit my job today. We're moving." And again, he lifted her off her feet and began waltzing about the room.

Stunned, Kitty gasped. "You what? Put me down. What did you say?"

Phil stood before her beaming with elation. His whole countenance had changed. He looked ready to conquer the world—confident, assured—qualities she hadn't sensed in him in months. But now, the old Phil was back. Standing before her was the enthusiastic, vibrant man she had married.

Realizing the knife she had been using when Phil suddenly swept her off her feet, was still in her hand, Kitty turned to place it on the counter. "Phil, what's going on? What are you talking about."

"Remember the job in Oregon I talked about some time ago, the position as the city's arborist? You were engrossed with some project you were working on for the magazine at the time, so we didn't get into a lot of details, but the more I thought about Oregon and the possibilities the job offered, the more interested I became. You know I've always hoped to move back West again, sometime. Anyway, when the Dean announced they were bringing Benson into the department, I became more and more certain I was about to be eased out. Oh, sure, I'm tenured. I could go on for years, performing the same old routine I've been doing. I didn't say anything to you 'cause I didn't want to get your hopes up until I knew more about the possibilities. Anyway, a couple of weeks ago, I decided it wouldn't hurt to pursue the situation, see if they'd filled the post yet. One thing led to another and today they called me, made an offer, and I accepted. We're moving to Oregon."

Her own big announcement forgotten, Kitty looked at Phil, really looked at him, and as she did it occurred to her that in recent months an ever-widening distance had come between them. With the twins away at college, she busy with her own activities and job, Phil muddling along as usual, each of them involved with his own affairs, it seemed as if out of habit, they lived side by side but not together. Sure they talked, compared schedules, discussed finances when necessary, kept in touch with the kids, still snuggled when they went to bed, but was that what she wanted for a life?

Evenings after dinner they turned on the TV. Phil, a multi-tasker, held the remote simultaneously reading and watching, randomly switching from channel to channel never landing in any one place long enough to capture her attention. Unable to concentrate with the TV on, she resorted to knitting or some other mindless task, or simply gave up and went to bed to pursue her own reading until Phil joined her. What kind of life was that? Certainly not what she had planned or hoped for when they married. And now this!

Phil's news had knocked her for a loop. One minute she'd been riding high, sure of herself, sure of the direction her life was taking, but now?

Stunned by Phil's unexpected announcement, Kitty fumbled for words. The buzzing of the oven timer saved her. Turning to check the potato casserole delayed the need to respond. "We'll talk about this later, but for now you'd better go wash up. Dinner's almost ready, and I'd like to eat while it's hot," and she popped the broiler pan with the lamb chops into the oven. "You can tell me more about this while we eat."

\* \* \* \*

Long after Phil fell asleep, Kitty lay beside him, her mind in a whirl as round and round the events of the day spun in her mind. What to do? Why hadn't she told Phil of her own big news? Rigid and separated she lay there, distanced in both physical space and spirit from her usual spot close to

Phil's warm back. How dare he—even if he thought he was protecting her—doing her a favor—trying to save her worry! What was he really thinking, or was he thinking at all? To pull a stunt like that—not even tell her before he accepted the job. Angrily she readjusted the pillow under her head and turned again to further widen the distance between them. The sound of Phil's steady breathing infuriated her. How could he just fall asleep?

Gradually her own breathing steadied, as spent and tired, her body released some of the oppressive anger, dropping from a raging boil to a slow simmer. She loved Phil. It was wonderful to see him so enthusiastic and happy again, but at what expense? Always the peacemaker, she hated conflict and quarreling, but why hadn't she told him about her own big news?

# Chapter 2

*P*hil woke early the next morning, and quietly slipped from the bed. The way Kitty had clung to her own side of the bed during the night had not gone unnoticed. He knew she was upset, but it had been a long week; maybe she was just tired, and now he'd had time to think about it, the news of his decision to take the job in Oregon must have come as a bit of a shock. This being Saturday, he pulled on a pair of jeans and a sweatshirt, trying not to disturb her slumber, and headed for the kitchen.

It was a glorious day, sunny and warm, a perfect morning to sit outside, sip a second cup of coffee, read the morning paper, and relax awhile. Soon after they moved to the big old house where they'd lived these many years, they'd converted the old narrow back porch that opened off the kitchen to a screened-in summer room. The family enjoyed many of their meals there, and that was where Kitty found him when she finally emerged from the bedroom.

Unlike her husband, Kitty was a morning person. Once out of bed, she was normally up and instantly ready to go, but this morning was different. Still in her robe, she poured herself a cup of coffee and stepped out to join Phil on the porch.

"Greetings sunshine. Glorious day, isn't it." Phil welcomed her company.

Not yet fully recovered from her midnight ruminations, and always one to get right to the point when she had something on her mind, Kitty barely smiled as she pulled out a chair and joined him at the table. "Phil, we need to talk." Kitty turned her chair to better look directly into her husband's face. "Put down the newspaper, please. And turn off that blasted radio! I've something to say, and it's important."

Startled by the unexpected tone of her voice, Phil did as she asked and waited. "Yes?" He waited some more.

Where to begin now she had his attention. Taking a deep breath, Kitty began, "Remember how excited you were when you came home last night with your big news? By any chance did you notice ... did you wonder why I'd made such a special effort with dinner? Why I'd splurged for lamb chops and a fancy dessert, put candles on the table? It was wonderful to see you so excited and enthusiastic, and I'm truly happy for you, but... When you took me in your arms and swung me in the air, you swept me off my feet in more ways than one."

"What are you getting at?" A hint of impatience, or was it uncertainty colored Phil's words.

Unused to openly expressing herself like this, Kitty hesitantly plowed on. "Okay. The thing is, I had some big news of my own to celebrate. I'd not only fixed a special dinner, I'd even bought champagne, but—"

"What do you mean? Why didn't you say something?"

"You didn't give me a chance, didn't even notice anything was different around you. Oh, Phil. It was wonderful to see you so thrilled with your own news. I didn't want to dull your enthusiasm and excitement. I knew you'd been frustrated at the University, but until that moment I hadn't realized how much it had changed you. Guess I'd been too busy, too concerned with my own life, to appreciate what you were going through. I've really enjoyed my work at the magazine. It's been good for me to get out in the work force again. Made me feel like I was doing something worthwhile for a change. It's helped me grow. I'm not "just a housewife" anymore. But there's a problem. Yesterday, Ed called me in to his office to offer an assignment I've wanted since before I even went back to work. It means a chance to get my name recognized as a journalist, to advance my career; it even involves a pay raise. The thing is, if I take the assignment, I have to be here in Maine, and... Oh, Phil, what should I do? I don't want anything to come between us. I love you and want only the best for you, but..."

"Whoa. What are you telling me? What do you mean come between us?"

"No, no. Don't get me wrong. It's just—oh, why must life get so complicated? If only you'd talked with me before you quit your job here and decided to move clear across the country. And what about the kids? We can't expect them to just pack up and follow us."

Stunned by this outburst, Phil sat there, silent, shaking his head. Then, without a word, he got up and left the table

* * * *

Following their conversation, Phil picked up his briefcase and left for his office—something he rarely did on a Saturday. Kitty dressed, and without bothering to eat, silently went about her usual Saturday chores. Lunchtime came and went. Phil did not return. Hungry by now, Kitty opened a can of soup, made herself a peanut-butter sandwich, ate, and leaving the pan of soup on the stove for Phil to find, she left for her usual Saturday shopping trip. As always, there were errands to run, and it was late afternoon before she returned. As she entered the house sounds of the television and a rousing ballgame greeted her. Placing her shopping bags on the kitchen counter, she wandered into the den. "I'm home," she called and Phil momentarily glanced away from the screen to acknowledge her greeting, then immediately turned to catch the action as his favorite player scored another run. No use trying to gain his attention now, Kitty realized, and she turned to the kitchen to store the week's purchase of groceries away.

The pan of soup she'd left on the stove for Phil's lunch sat on the burner, untouched, just as she had left it. Had Phil eaten? she wondered. No doubt he's hungry, but tired now, both physically and emotionally, she didn't feel like cooking, and taking a pizza from the freezer she put it in the oven to warm. They'd eat in front of the television tonight, something they rarely did, but tonight was different. She sensed the chill of uncertainty, and uncomfortable silence that lay between them—none of the usual cheering or sparring that usually engaged them as they each rooted for their favorite players or panned the opposing team, while watching a game together. Silence reigned and it was apparent the morning's breakfast conversation was not forgotten.

Finishing her pizza, Kitty picked up their plates, took them to the kitchen and tidied the kitchen. Then, instead of rejoining Phil, she retired to the bedroom, attended to her usual bedtime rituals, picked up the new novel she' purchased that afternoon, and crawled into bed to read. Yet her mind kept straying back to the problem that plagued her. What to do? What should she tell Ed on Monday morning? And what was Phil thinking? Unable to concentrate on her book, she dimmed the bedside light and resigned herself to try to sleep.

* * * *

Ballgame over, Phil quietly slipped into the bedroom. It hadn't even been a good ballgame, but what was there to say, what to do? All day long earlier events of the week had clouded his mind, even as he struggled to prepare to move ahead with his decision to move. It hadn't been easy to write his letter of resignation from the University—especially after Kitty's reaction that morning, but he had done it. Deep inside, he was convinced this decision was right, not just for him, but for Kitty, too. Surely, in time she'd get used to the idea, and the job in Oregon was a great opportunity. More than anything Kitty and the kids were the most important things in his life, but... I thought she would be pleased, that it would be a fun surprise. Why hadn't she told me her work at the magazine wasn't just a job, what it really meant to her? How was I to know? When she went back to work, all she said was that she needed something to do now that the kids were grown. Besides, aren't I supposed to be the breadwinner, the head of the family, the one responsible to care for them all?

Phil crawled into bed and his hand tenderly reached for Kitty's. Strong and familiar, the warmth of his touch said more than words, and half asleep, Kitty drew close. Silently they lay there, bound together as each in his own way searched for answers to bind them together as separately they reached for solutions to bridge the gap that lay between them.

\* \* \* \*

Ten minutes after arriving at the office Monday morning, Kitty approached Ed's door. Might as well get this over with, even though she wasn't yet quite sure what she wanted to tell him. Thank heavens he was one of those bosses one could talk to whether about personal problems or work, someone who acted more like a friend—one of the crew, than a distant tyrant. But always, there was no doubt who was in charge, who controlled the purse strings. Gently, she knocked on his door.

"Ed, something happened after I left here Friday night. I'm sure you know how thrilled I was when you told me you'd decided to go ahead with the family life and home stories I proposed so long ago, but..." Kitty fidgeted in her chair as she spoke, uncertain, hesitant to reveal the rift that had opened between her and her husband.

"What's the matter, Kitty? Is something wrong?" He motioned for Kitty to sit in the chair before him. "Don't you want to do the series?"

"You know I do, but when I got home Friday night, before I could even mention my news, Phil hit me with a surprise of his own. For a long time he's been frustrated with the way things are going at the University. However, I wasn't aware he was secretly trying to do something about it. He wanted to spare me, I guess. Anyway, Friday night he announced he had accepted a job in Oregon."

"Wow, what a surprise! I thought the two of you were here for life, that you were as permanent a part of Maine as the lobsters we're noted for. That's one reason I put you in charge of the Family Matters section when I did. Move? Hmm..."

"So did I, but ... sometimes things change, I guess. I'm told even the lobster beds aren't as sure a thing as they once were. Oh, Ed, what should I do? I love it here. This is where my heart is. This is home—where I've lived for over twenty years. And it's home to the kids. They decided to enroll in State College instead of someplace else so they'd be close to home. If I had my way I'd continue to live here for the rest of my life, but Phil has always wanted to go West again— he grew up in Idaho, you know—and isn't it a wife's place to follow her husband? You know that line 'wherever thou goest, I shalt go.' I grew up never questioning that. But now, I don't know what to do. I want to do the series, to interview Maine families, but to do the job I have to be in Maine." Kitty's voice dwindled off as she spoke. Her posture slumped and she found herself on the verge of tears.

Ed came to her rescue. "Well, you don't have to make a decision right this minute. Let's give it a few days, give you a chance to get used to the idea, then we'll talk again. I appreciate your coming to me now, however, instead of waiting to tell me after I'd plotted things out for the new year. Go back to work now, and try to put this quandary on the back burner for awhile. I'm sure you and Phil will manage to work things out." Ed rose, and giving her shoulder an understanding pat, opened the office door to usher her out.

* * * *

Back at her desk, Kitty opened her daybook, considered the list of things to be done today, but her mind was elsewhere. Why is this so difficult? Why can't life just go on and on? I thought we were settled. Life was slowing down now the kids are almost grown and away from home. Is it age that's brought this on? And then she laughed at herself as she thought of her name. Kitty. What a silly childish name for a grown up woman like me. She'd been called Kitty since she was an infant. A sweet cuddly name for a youngster but was that how people thought of her? Over the years there had been times when some other nickname caught on for awhile—Katy, Kit, Kate—but invariably it was Kitty that hung around.

Kitty, she thought to herself. Sounds like some pet to be loved and protected or shunted about according to the whim of the moment. Does Phil thinks of me that way, like one of the family pets, always to be counted on to follow him about? For that matter, what do I think of myself? Aren't my wants and needs just as important as his?

Momentarily, anger flared. Huffily she rose from her chair and, mug in hand, stomped off to the coffee machine to bolster herself with a jolt of caffeine. But the memories of her past wouldn't stop reeling in her mind. Too many changes happening all at once. For years she'd chosen to be a stay-at-home Mom. Then five years ago when the twins were still in high school she'd gone back to work. She'd worked hard to reclaim the status she'd held before Julie and Johnny were born. The work gave new purpose to life. But now that, too, would change. Her past and this opportunity would both be left behind. Moving meant starting all over again to build a reputation, reestablish an identity, and this time there would be no contacts, no connections, and a totally new environment. Kitty, Kathy, Kate or Katherine. Who am I? What am I? And where is life taking me, she worried.

* * * *

Somehow she got through the day, even managed to get a little work done. She completed her article for next month's issue and even planned ahead for the special Christmas edition they put out each year. Keeping busy helped forestall the problems awaiting her at home. Marla caught her just before noon. "How about joining me for lunch in the cafeteria? I've a couple of ideas I need to talk over with someone." So they lunched, and Marla aired the layout she was designing. Strictly a business lunch and no time for Kitty to even think about sharing her own concerns.

But when her work day ended, it all lay before her again, and there was no way to avoid the issue. Phil was home early for once, waiting for her. "I thought we might go out for dinner tonight. Give you a break. You seemed pretty distraught this morning. How did it go today?" he asked. "Did you talk with Ed?"

"Yes, and he was good about it, but we didn't come up with any solutions except for me to think it over and talk with you. The offer to do the series still stands. How about you? What did the Dean have to say?"

Phil went to the refrigerator, took out the bottle of wine they'd opened the previous night and poured a glass for each of them. They sat down at the kitchen table, the place where most family issues were discussed. "He was surprised, of course, wants me to stay on until the end of summer school, which I planned to do anyway. That way they can advertise and should have someone to take my place in time for winter quarter. I'd be free to start on the job in Oregon about the first of September. Would this work for you?"

So many details to consider. They finished their wine and walked down to Jerry's, a small, neighborhood restaurant. The atmosphere was quiet there so they could talk and the food was simple but good. By the end of the evening they'd worked out a plan.

Both of the twins had summer jobs, but they would be home to spend some time before enrolling for their junior year. "Could you perhaps start the interview process for the series you want to write and then maybe finish it up after we move?" Phil asked. Gradually they worked out a possible compromise. It would mean being separated for awhile, but maybe it would work. Phil would go to Oregon ahead of her. She'd stay in Maine—list their house for sale and tend to the closing of affairs here while Phil started on his new job and found them a place to live out there. Perhaps Ed could assign someone to work on the series with her who would then be able to take over and continue after she was gone. At least she would have the opportunity to do an introductory article or two to establish the format.

# Chapter 3

The days that followed fairly whirled by—so many things to attend to, so many farewells to face. Phil moved ahead, excited, thrilled, looking forward. For Kitty it was a different story. One moment she was up, the next she slipped into despair. Friends helped bolster her optimism, supported her when she was down. And Madge—what would she do without her good and faithful neighbor who called to her over the fence, dropped by with a plate of cookies, and listened to her tales of woe with such an understanding ear. And it was wonderful when the kids came home, even if it was for only a couple of weeks in August. They made the most of those days, the four of them doing things together. Picnic suppers in the back yard, an overnight visit to their favorite camping spot along the coast, and then it was time for Johnny and Julie to prepare to leave for school again. The true significance of the distance that would lie between them suddenly hit home. Oregon seemed so far away.

And then Phil left. For the first time in twenty-five years, Kitty was alone. The big old Victorian house echoed about her. So quiet. No kids racing up and down the stairs, no rock music vibrating from their bedroom walls, no tennis rackets or sweaty athletic shoes cluttering up the place, no Phil calling down the stairs, 'where did you put my socks?' And her usual answer, 'did you look in your drawer?' She could swear, even after all these years, he was as helpless as a newborn kitten. But oh, how she missed those little annoyances.

Each day she went to work. Each evening she came home alone. Ed had agreed to let her plan and begin the series of interviews. Lila, a new girl who had started as a summer intern, worked with her, and it was going well. Lila was young, anxious to learn and a good photographer whose pictures complemented well the script they'd devised to follow. Their first story would come out in the January issue—about the same time as she would be leaving, but in the mean time it was a thrill to be doing the kind of reporting she'd always hoped to do. Maybe, if these first stories went over well, they'd help her land a new job in Oregon. Or maybe she wouldn't get a regular job right away—try her hand as a freelance writer for awhile. Who knew? A whole new future lay before her, a grand adventure as Madge kept reminding her.

Then there were other days. As the bright, sunny days of autumn began to chill, the trees lost their Jacob's coats of gold and red, blustery winds rustled the season away, and her spirits fell along with the leaves. Loss. Her old life, friends, the house she loved, the home she'd labored to create, along with her job—all would be gone. Left behind for an unknown future.

"Everything is always green and beautiful in Oregon," Phil reassured her, "even in January." He remembered a Christmas card he'd received from a high school buddy who was living there at the time. He'd told about mowing his lawn on Christmas day. So what, she'd asked, as she looked out at the two feet of snow covering their yard. Who'd want to mow a lawn on Christmas day anyway?

The first month after Phil left was especially hard, but eventually she began to adjust. In some ways it was rather nice to have her independence—to be able to join the rest of the crew for a drink and bit of chat after work—nice to pick up a carton of soup or some other goodie from the deli instead of rushing home to prepare the usual meat and potatoes Phil preferred. But, oh, how cold the bed sheets felt as she crawled in alone each night without Phil there to reach for her hand or draw her into his strong, warm arms as he whispered, 'night Kitten.' Just thinking of such moments of tenderness brought her back to reality, reemphasized the loneliness she was experiencing during these months of separation.

Kitten. Only Phil called her that, and only in private moments, just as she sometimes called him "Phlip." The little private joke between them had started when Julie first tried to write her Daddy's name. All those P's and L's were a bit too much, and it came out P-H-L-I-P, so Phlip had been her private name for him ever since. And a 'flip' was what Phil had done when he came home that Friday to announce he'd quit his job.

In October, the kids came home for a three-day weekend. When was it? Columbus Day? While they were home she started them going through their stuff, deciding what treasures they wanted to keep, what to dispose of when they actually moved. It was time for them all to face up to the reality of what was coming. Busy though she was, all the sifting and sorting was a job she'd have to tackle soon, and after twenty years the house was crammed full of mementos and memories. It was when Julie and Johnny left to return to the campus that the full impact of what lay ahead really touched her. In Oregon, there'd be no more of these brief holiday visits. Maybe they could afford for the twins to fly out for Christmas and Spring Break, but even with Phil's boost in salary there would be limits.

Time wore on. Her work on the family series progressed nicely. She and Lisa had devised an outline of topics to be included as they interviewed each family—income level, housing, choice of locale, career, family roles, interests, hobbies, etc. Most of all, they tried to develop a feel for priorities and values that influenced each family's life choices. Already they'd collected data for three stories, and she'd started to write. She was encouraged. All seemed to be going well, and Lisa was a jewel to work with. A former college sociology major, she was full of ideas. What's more, she was quick to adapt from academic writing to the less formal tone of the magazine. Maybe Lisa could become the *Family Matters* columnist when she left. She'd have to talk with Ed—start grooming Lisa if he agreed.

Then suddenly it was November. Christmas décor sprung up everywhere, Salvation Army bells jingled, Santas obnoxiously ho-ho-hoed at every turn. Long before Thanksgiving she was sick of it all. The time pressures of the holiday season descended. She didn't need that right now. Already there was more to do than she could possibly accomplish. As usual, Madge came to the rescue and invited her and the kids to have Thanksgiving dinner at her home. Her sons and their families would be coming this year—a rare treat in itself. They lived some distance away. Phil would be staying in Corvallis, but he planned to come home for Christmas and help prepare for the move.

The house was listed with the realtor but so far there hadn't been a lot of showings. Not the best time of year to sell, the agent emphasized, but he'd do his best. On Friday afternoon Kitty's office phone rang. "Mrs. Lundstrom, this is Charlie Duncan from the realty office. I have a couple arriving tomorrow who are planning to move here. They'll only be in the area for a few days. I know this could be inconvenient for you, but they'd like to see your house on Thanksgiving day. Would that be possible? I don't usually work on holidays, but in this case..." He went on and on about how her house seemed to be exactly what they were looking for, what lovely people they seemed to be, a family of four, a perfect fit, etc. etc. And as he talked Kitty's mind spun. The kids would get home Wednesday night; they were all invited out for Thanksgiving dinner and she could spiff the place up the previous Saturday. In the end she agreed.

Then on Tuesday morning all hell broke loose. She'd worked late at the office Monday evening determined to finish up the first draft for the second story of the series— this one about the O'Malley family who had moved to the area from Texas a year ago. "That must have been a shock," Kitty remarked to Mrs. O'Malley during their interview, to which her interviewee simply replied, 'that's military life.' Lieutenant O'Malley was a navy recruiter. Anyway, it was almost nine when Kitty arrived home, and there was a message from Phil on the answering machine asking her to call as soon as she got in.

He'd finally found a house that interested him, one he was sure she, too, would like. It was located in a fairly new neighborhood and overlooked a natural wooded area at the rear of the house. The family living there would be leaving the first of the year; the asking price was within their means. Could she possibly get away to come see it with him over the weekend? What to do?

The kids were to arrive the next day, she was swamped at the office, and Madge was expecting them for Thanksgiving dinner. Everything was happening at once. And then Tuesday morning when she was still only half-awake, she padded into the kitchen to start the coffee and found herself sloughing through an inch of water. The old sheepskin slippers she wore were soaked.

Over the years, the foundation of their old Victorian house had settled. The floor at one end of the room had sunk so it now sloped to about an inch lower than the rest of the kitchen. That whole section was flooded. The floor over by the sink was afloat. Shedding her soggy slippers Kitty dashed to the bathroom, grabbed an armload of towels, ran back to the kitchen and began to mop up the wet. Where was the water coming from? Where was the shut-off valve? Oh where was Phil when she needed him?

She kneeled to look at the array of pipes under the sink, and as she opened the cabinet doors, another flood of water spilled across the room, soaking the bottom of her robe and nightgown as it did. Oh, no! Stepping back to the dry floor Kitty dropped to her knees and began to sob. Too much! She couldn't take anymore. Crying helped, and as the flood of tears gradually diminished, she looked at the situation and began to laugh. Ridiculous. All her weekend effort to get the house in perfect order to show and now this.

At 8 o'clock she called the plumbing shop. They'd send someone out as soon as possible to locate the problem and find the shut off valve, but it would be tomorrow at least before they could have anyone available to do any major repair work. Meanwhile, 'for heaven's sake, don't try to use the sink or dishwasher,' the desk girl reminded her. So much for cleaning up. What she needed right now was a strong cup of coffee. So carafe in hand, she headed for the bathroom to fill the pot. While the coffee brewed, she called the office to explain what had happened. She'd be in as soon as possible, but who knew when that would be. And, so much for flying to Oregon.

By nine o'clock she'd reached Phil to explain what was happening. Why don't you go ahead and deal with the house you've found, she proposed. At this point I might as well trust your judgment on that matter. Trust his judgment? Wasn't that what had placed them in this dilemma in the first place? Momentarily, resentment and anger overcame her as she recalled all the decisions she'd been forced to make. It wasn't just the big things like trying to sell the house, but other things, little things. She loved Phil, wanted him to be happy, successful, but why did he have to disrupt their lives so? Oh well, the house he'd found in Oregon was all new and modern, he explained, placing special emphasis on that word modern. By God, it had better be, she thought. No more broken pipes or whatever this was. She'd had it!

* * * *

The kids arrived home late Wednesday afternoon, and as always it was wonderful to be with them again. "What's happened?" Johnny asked, as he walked into the kitchen, hungry and ready to raid the refrigerator just like he always did. "What's that smell, and what are all the heaters and fans doing in here?"

So Kitty explained about the flood she'd had. "Luckily it was only a loose connection between the dishwasher drain and the sink, but a lot of water spilled. I'm trying to get the place dried out before the house viewing appointment that's to take place Thanksgiving Day."

It was almost dinnertime by then, but she didn't even

comment as Johnny poured himself a second glass of milk and snatched a couple more cookies from the cookie jar. She'd baked the night before. Julie was on the phone in the other room, already back in touch with her best friend, Rachel, who was also home for the holiday.

Kitty turned on the oven and started it heating to warm the lasagna she'd brought from the deli for their supper that night. She'd planned to make up a batch from her own recipe, but with all the confusion the day before she'd run out of time. Shaw's Supermarket best would have to do. While she and Johnny visited, she prepared ingredients for a green salad, and set the French bread out to slice for garlic toast—one of Johnny's favorites.

"How's Dad getting along?" Johnny asked. "Does he like his new job?"

"He seems to. Says he's keeping plenty busy. Lots to catch up on, the position having been vacant for so long. And it seems that a year ago they had a devastating ice storm that broke a lot of trees and uprooted others. The concern is that these will become diseased and infect the healthy ones left standing. Corvallis is supposed to be renowned for its lovely shade trees. Your dad's in charge of protecting all that. But the big news is he thinks he's found a house that will accommodate us. He called Monday night and wanted me to come look at it with him, but with all that's going on here, I don't see how I can do that just now. Guess we'll all just have to trust his judgment and hope he's doing the right thing." (And please, God, let this be. I couldn't bear for him to get so down and discouraged as he has been these past two years, she silently prayed.) Then turning to Johnny, she added, "But now it's your turn. Tell me about you and all that's been going on in your life."

\* \* \* \*

Thanksgiving Day with Madge was perfect—well, as perfect as it could be without Phil there to join them. She served a delicious dinner and afterwards they all joined in cleaning up, then played a variety of table games. Madge's boys were avid domino players, and they introduced a new version of the popular Mexican Train game that all their friends were playing. With all of Madge's family present, there were fourteen of them for dinner, and Madge brought out a large enough set of dominoes so everyone could play— even the younger children. And along with the game, they all shared in an abundance of teasing and bantering.

Then before it seemed possible Thanksgiving was past and the holidays were upon them. Phil arrived three days before Christmas and gasped in shock at all the snow he found on the ground. "You mean you've forgotten winter in Maine already?" Johnny jibed and in turn teased his Dad about growing moss on his back. But Kitty just smiled and folded herself in his arms with a welcoming kiss.

The days flew by as they tried to incorporate all the old, familiar Christmas traditions into their last holiday in the 'home where they all grew up,' as Julie described it. The Christmas tree ornamented with its familiar angel on top and the funny peanut parrot ornaments Kitty had helped the children make the year she was a scout den mother assumed their usual places. The red and green striped socks she'd knit for each of them hung from the fireplace mantle as usual. The Dickensian Christmas pudding that only once had had enough brandy poured over it to actually burst into flame, was tried again this year and wonder of wonders its blue flame glowed in the evening dusk. And after dinner, while carols played on the stereo, Phil set up the slide projector and they watched their usual photo show of years gone by—Kitty and Phil on their honeymoon, baby pictures of the twins, birthdays and camping trips. Nostalgia reigned and more than once Kitty wiped a tear from her eye and noted that Phil swallowed and blew his nose a time or two as he paused in his narration of remembrances.

Then it was over. Phil left to go back to work, the kids returned to school, and Kitty was once more alone. Two days later, they had an offer on the house—the same people who had called for a showing Thanksgiving day while she and the children were dining at Madge's. Now the pressure was really on. So much more sifting and sorting and packing left to do. Papers to sign on the house sale, visits to the lawyer's office, the bank and through it all, the pressure to wind up the last of the first three segments of the series she was to finish for *Maine Scene*.

The days sped by, and knowing she would soon be leaving, invitation after invitation arrived—friends and associates wanting to say goodbye before she left. It was midnight most nights when, exhausted, she finally fell in to bed.

And then the time came. The movers arrived, packed up the last of the boxes, loaded the truck and drove off as Kitty stood on the front steps watching her past roll down the street.

That night she rolled out the air mattress she had retained as she planned to spend this final night in the home that for so long had meant so much to her. Tired though she was, long after crawling into bed she lay awake listening to the familiar creaks and groans as the January winds whistled and moaned around the corners of the house. All too soon the raucous, obnoxious squawking of the alarm clock blasted her from slumber. Morning's first light had not yet crept across the room, as disoriented and confused, she searched for the source of the noise. Finally, in a fit of desperation, she located the clock and sent it crashing to its death across the bare wooden floor. "Damn," she muttered. "Not already," and with a vehement tug she pulled the blanket over her head. Five minutes. Just five minutes more, then she'd get up and face the day. But the solace of sleep had passed.

Reluctantly, she slid from the makeshift bed, swung sock-covered feet to the floor, stuffed them in the ragged, sheepskin slippers that had been so thoroughly soaked only a month or so before and dragged herself to the bathroom. The last day. Then what? Bleary eyed, she stared at the image in her mirror. Bloodshot eyes stared back. No more tears. One more day and it would be over.

As if to scrub away the emotional turmoil that gripped

her, she vigorously splashed her face with icy water from the early morning tap. Calmer now, she wrapped herself in the warm fleecy robe that hung by the door and headed downstairs. The empty house echoed as she made her way to the kitchen, opened the faucet, filled the kettle and set it to boil. Turning to the cupboard where the everyday dishes normally sat, she lifted the one remaining bowl from the shelf, emptied the last of the Cornflakes into it, and headed to the refrigerator for the bottle of milk.

Breakfast over, she turned to the sink and automatically rinsed her bowl, crack and all, before dashing it in the trash. The satisfying sound of shattering pottery mimicked her mood as she dwelt on this shattering of her own life. Then, turning, she made herself another cup of instant coffee and shuffled from the room, slamming the kitchen door behind her. She couldn't help it; it wasn't fair. Phil had just waltzed off to start his new job, excited as a kid who'd finally got the pony he'd wished for on every birthday candle since he was four years old. He had left it up to her to sell the house, pack, decide what to take, what to leave behind.

Maybe she was just tired, exhausted was more like it, but this morning it was hard to look ahead positively. Once again she struggled to reconcile the decisions she'd made, parting with unnecessary items like excess books, seldom used dishes, and most difficult of all, sentimental items like the twins baby clothes, the cradle she'd saved for them to use when they had children of their own. A few things she refused to relinquish—Julie's Cabbage Patch doll, Johnny's fire-truck—gifts Santa had brought.   They were soiled, ragged and worn, and at this point they seemed to have little sentimental value to the children, but for her? Their new home would be smaller, Phil had told her, a comfortable house but without the attic space and extra rooms they'd enjoyed while the children were growing up. But somewhere she'd squeeze these keepsakes in. Nostalgia overcame her and a flood of memories once more passed before her eyes. How simple life had been back then when the children were little. Not a lot of money, Phil was only an assistant professor, but lot's of love and so much happiness had surrounded them all in this big old turn-of-the century house.

Momentarily, a warm feeling engulfed her as she thought of how Madge and her other friends had supported her through these last difficult months. Even good old Al, her office companion, had twice given up his usual Saturday afternoon football game to help Johnny with the heavy lifting as they prepared for the garage sale. She could never have managed without his help, not to mention Janie, Meg and Paula who had taken charge of the pre-sale pricing and then tended the cash box during the sale.

As Kitty crossed the front hall on her way to the bedroom, the first rays of sun struck the crystal panes of the leaded window at the head of the stairs casting diamond prisms of light across her path as she mounted the steps. Once again, tears moistened her eyes. That window—how she'd miss it. The brilliance of its light on the afternoon she and Phil first walked into this old Victorian relic was what had drawn them to the place. That was twenty years ago, and the magic of that twinkling light darting about the room had cast a glow of romance on their lives ever since. Tinker Bell's lantern the children called those moments when rainbows from its many panes sparkled and flickered about the room. Over and over the children begged her to read the story of Peter Pan. She was Wendy. They the lost boys.

Those days were long past now, but she remembered, and so did they. Just the weekend before, on their last visit home, Julie had talked of how they'd snuggled in the big chair by the fireplace and watched that magic light. What would become of memories like that now? Would the new house in Oregon ever seem like home to them? Again tears brimmed her eyes as she thought of the miles that would separate the family. Here, the college was only one hundred miles away, but now? Now, they'd be clear across the country?

What would the house Phil had selected for them really be like, she wondered. Different, he had explained, all

shiny and almost new. Why hadn't she gone when he said
he'd found something? Surely she could have arranged it
somehow after the Thanksgiving weekend. Why had she
felt the assignment she was on more important, that she
owed it to the magazine to stay, meet the deadline, fulfill her
contract, be at her job every day to the bitter end? Too late
now. That chance was past.

Opening the closet door she took out her trusty, red suit.
No drab black today. Perhaps some color would cheer her
up, help hide her misgivings about the move, make it easier
to pretend that all was well and good. What was it? Did she
simply resent change, or was there reason for her concern
about the choices Phil had made as they entered this new
stage of life? Would he be able to handle this new job? Would
it reinvigorate him, renew his self esteem?

She really was in a bad way this morning. For months now
she'd been going along, making the best of the situation, but
today—was it cold feet, stage fright, fear of the unknown?

Shame on you, she chided herself. This isn't the time to
be second-guessing your husband. Your role is to trust, to
believe, to encourage him, to help him achieve the success
that is so important to him.

Her friends seemed to think it was the empty nest
syndrome that was bothering her. Little did they know. The
family nest would be empty all right with the twins back
here at school, but— the problem was distance. There'd be
only herself, Phil, and the Oregon rain, miles away. But even
that was not what really concerned her. Other folks adjusted
to these changes every day, and so would she. Nor was it just
Phil. It was private things, secret doubts about herself that
really bothered her.

Oh well, no time to dwell on that now. Glancing in the
mirror, she added a blush of color to her cheeks, swiped a
line of crimson lipstick across her lips, and dashed for the
car. With luck she might even get to the office on time today.
Today, her last day. Then what?

# Chapter 4

*H*uddled in the corner of her window seat on the plane, Kitty averted her eyes from the other boarding passengers, fixed her gaze instead on the tarmac below and pretended to watch the loading of luggage. She was grateful for the window seat. If only the seat next to her would remain vacant for this trip. Just now she didn't feel like talking with anyone. Quietly she sighed, letting herself relax, forcing the tension of the last few days to flow from her body. Doing so, the package Madge had casually stuffed in her open carryon as they parted slipped to the floor. Bending over to pick it up, she realized that in the confusion of parting she had barely acknowledged the gift. Madge, always the thoughtful one. Oh, how she would miss her kind and caring ways. She always seemed to know just what Kitty was feeling, to understand and offer wise words of counsel. So what had she come up with this time?

Just then a portly businessman dropped a laptop computer on the seat beside her as he hoisted an oversize bag into the bin above Kitty's head. He removed his suitcoat and loosened his tie, then plopped into the aisle seat, and reached for his laptop. He smiled, briefly acknowledging her presence, then without speaking a word proceeded to get to work. Good, now if only someone else doesn't claim that seat between us, I'll have my wish, Kitty thought as she resumed her study of the tarmac and the now empty luggage cart below. Looked like they'd soon be on their way. She leaned back, closed her eyes, and waited for the plane to roll down the runway. Only then did she realize how tired she really was.

As the plane idled, the flight attendant went through her preflight instructions. Then the engines roared, propelling the plane down the runway and into the air.

Kitty's thoughts turned to Madge. She'd had dinner and spent the last night at her house. They'd talked until midnight. Her car was temporarily parked in Madge's extra garage space. One of the twins would come pick it up next weekend. How excited they were when she told them she was leaving it for their use. Oregon was too long a drive to make alone this time of year. The plan was for the children to bring it out and spend their spring break in Oregon. Meanwhile, she hoped they'd be careful and use the common sense she and Phil tried to instill in them. After all, it was still her car. Oh, how she hoped they could come. Despite what Phil kept telling her about loosing the apron strings, they were still just kids, and she so wanted them to think of home as being with Phil and her, wherever they were.

Her thoughts returned to Madge. What would she do without her? They'd been friends and neighbors for over ten years. Funny, the way they'd met. Wouldn't you know, it was the same day Johnny made his first home run for the little league ball team; in his exuberance afterward he'd persuaded Julie to pitch him a ball in the backyard and whack, he scored another hit, right through Madge's kitchen window. Shame-faced and fearful, he dropped his bat and ran for Kitty. How many times had he been told not to hit the ball hard in their little back yard? He was sorry, so he and Kitty went over together to confront Madge.

Johnny apologized, offered to pay for fixing the window out of his allowance, if only she'd let him do it on installments—he was sure he wouldn't have enough money all at once. Fortunately, Madge had three sons of her own, all grown now; she was understanding but firm. Yes, she'd let him pay a little at a time, and perhaps she could even find a job or two for him to do in lieu of cash. From then on she, Johnny, and Madge had become friends. And last night the two of them had talked for hours, recalling happy memories, laughing at past antics, remembering and remembering as they reminisced. Then they'd talked of the future. Madge mentioned again what life had been for her when she first moved into the neighborhood. It hadn't been easy. She was in a situation somewhat like Kitty was in now. Her last child gone from home, she without a job after spending the last twenty years as "just a housewife." Then her husband had asked for a divorce. The last thing in the world she ever expected was to be a divorced woman. That was the hardest part, but look at her now—she'd managed, and had come out a stronger, better person for it. Life was good, and she had found wonderful friends—friends like Kitty, Phil and the twins, not to mention the multitude of others who regularly frequented her life. "You'll be fine," she reassured when Kitty admitted her reluctance to leave, to give up the life she knew.

"Think of it as a grand new adventure," Madge advised. "Why, just think of all the marvelous and unexpected things that have come my way in the years since I've lived next door to you. Like the job I found as receptionist at the visitor's center, the dignitaries and other people I met as a result. That was where I first met Emma Bruins. How excited I was when she asked me to work on her campaign the year she ran for the legislature. My experience as a displaced homemaker fit right in with her campaign."

Kitty sighed as she recalled this conversation. Yes, an adventure her new life in Oregon would be. Closing this line of thought, Kitty reached down and lifted Madge's package from her carryon. What might it be? She shook it, and felt the sharp edges of a gift box. Then gently, being careful not to destroy the pretty paper and ribbon, Kitty unwrapped the package and raised the lid. *Thoughts for Today,* gold lettering inscribed on a simple, leather-bound book. Lifting the gift from its box, Kitty thumbed the pages. Blank. And then she discovered Madge's card and note tucked inside the cover.

*Kitty, my friend,*

*I know you are facing this next stage of life with some trepidation. But trust yourself, my dear, and when you have concerns, reach for this little book. Let it be the friend you count on. It is your private book, yours alone to read. You are a writer, you've proved it professionally; now prove it in your personal life. As you record here both the joys and uncertainties of your days, may it lead you to analyze, to better know yourself. Feel free to vent, let emotions roll. Question, explore, dream. Let this book help you understand who you are, what you are, and what you want to be.*

*Best wishes my dear. You know my thoughts and wishes for your welfare come with this book. Until we again meet and have an evening to share—*

*Love always,*
*Madge*

Dabbing a tear from her cheek, Kitty returned the book to its box. Her own journal? Well, she'd see. Maybe, someday she'd give it a try. Suddenly, she yawned. The effect of last night's short hours of sleep was taking its toll. Reaching for the small airline pillow, she stuffed it in the corner between seat and window, and laid her head back. A little sleep while flying would feel good and help pass the hours.

* * * *

They were somewhere over the Dakotas when Kitty awoke. The stewardess was just handing her seatmate a glass of Pepsi. "Oh, you are awake. You appeared to be sleeping so soundly I wasn't going to disturb you." The pleasant looking young woman smiled and added, "Could I serve you something?"

Sensing the dryness of her mouth after sleeping, Kitty managed to whisper. "A glass of ice water would be nice, and a cup of hot coffee if you have one."

"Coming right up," the stewardess responded as she emptied ice into a glass, opened a bottle of water and handed it to Kitty. "I'll have your coffee just as soon as I serve the rest of my passengers."

Kitty thanked her, took a sip of water, and for the first time since she'd boarded the plane really became aware of the other passengers around her. Again she looked out the window. The sky was clear, sunlight poured into the plane. Sunshine helped. Already she was feeling better, a little more ready to tackle her new life. It would be good to be with Phil again. How long before they would land? He was to meet her in Portland, then drive them to Corvallis so she could get the feel of the country.

Awake now, Kitty straightened her clothes, took out a comb and fluffed her hair from where she was sure it had flattened as she slept. Through the window, even at this elevation, she could catch glimpses of the landscape below. We must be flying over the badlands, she thought. That would mean about two, maybe three more hours, and they would be there. The hostess arrived with her coffee and a snack-pack of pretzels. Good, the coffee was nice and hot, just what she needed. The pretzels she popped in her carryon. She and Phil could share them some evening with a before dinner glass of wine.

Phil? She felt that unmistakable tingle at the very thought of seeing him. Would he have changed in the months they'd been apart? Had he been getting enough to eat? He never was much of a cook. That was basically her job.

She began to wonder about the house he'd picked out for them. He'd said it was new, modern. Modern? What did that mean? Not one of those stainless steel and glass models, she hoped. Surely by now he realized that was not her style. She liked things warm and cozy, casual, an eclectic mix, a friendly place where everyone felt free to relax and be himself. Oh, it would be fun to get to do some decorating again. She had a flare for the artistic, if she did say so herself. She enjoyed the creative challenge of choosing colors, arranging pictures and all the little personal things that made a house a home. When she'd asked how their old furniture worked in the house, Phil had just sort of grunted, and said, "I'll leave that for you to decide. You know that isn't my forte." Quite naturally their furnishings showed the usual signs of wear and tear that occur during twenty-three years of marriage and family life. Maybe it was time for some changes. They'd be living in a college town, where people often discarded perfectly good sofas and such when they moved or went on sabbatical. Maybe she could find a delightful consignment or second hand store like Marie mentioned finding when they moved. Actually, that might be fun. She really was tired of that old, faded-green couch. Perhaps it was time for a change in more ways than one.

Maybe she wouldn't try to go back to work for awhile, give herself time to adjust, explore the community and see what it had to offer. Phil's salary was greater now, and even in the past they'd tried to set most of her income aside as savings to be used to play with when they retired. Retired? Seemed funny to be thinking of that now just as they were starting on this new venture. Let's see, if Phil worked until he was sixty-five that only gave him twelve more years. No wonder he was feeling the pressure to gain the recognition, the proof of success that seemed so important to him—as if he had to prove himself. But what did success mean? What was his standard of measurement? She knew he was a good man, hard working, had always been loyal, true and faithful to her, the kids and his job. What more did he want?

He is a good man, she again reminded herself, and I mustn't let him down, not now. In spite of what others may think, I still feel that if a marriage is to work it's the wife's role to put her own wishes aside and stand beside her husband. She recalled how on the day of her wedding, Grandma offered her words of guidance, reminding her that such was the foundation for a happy marriage. She'd taken those words to heart, and even though many of her friends thought her attitude out of step with the times, she'd clung to that basic principle. Recalling this now she felt a twinge of guilt, shame. Had she been selfish in not having been more enthusiastic when Phil seemed so excited and enthused about this great new opportunity? She'd do her best to remember, make it up to him now, maintain a positive attitude, and think of the new life she was beginning as the grand adventure Madge suggested. Together, she and Phil would make it all work out. Everything would be fine.

\* \* \* \*

As Kitty exited the tunnel from the plane her eyes searched for Phil. He wasn't there. Then she remembered the new security regulation—only ticket holders allowed beyond the security check. Admittedly disappointed at not finding him waiting, she continued on with the long line of departing passengers. Finally, there he was, his six foot three inch stance looming head and shoulders above the other greeters. He stood at the rear of the crowd, patient, considerate as usual, to accommodate those shorter than he. Their eyes met as she scurried ahead, and he shouldered his way to meet her.

"Kit, Kit. You're here at last. Can you even begin to guess how much I've missed you." His words shrank the distance between them as he wrapped her in his arms, and she relaxed, steadied by the familiar touch, the familiar scent of his after-shave. Yes, all was well. She'd be okay.

Slowly he released her, but just enough that he might hold her at arm's length, as if to make sure she was really there. Where to begin? So much to talk about, so much to share. And then they both spoke at once, laughed as if to say, whose turn first? Once more they both started to speak. He was anxious to show her their new home, eager for her to see his new place of work. He hoped she'd like the neighborhood. The urgency of his voice begged for her to like it all as much as he did. She focused on his words, marveling at this talkativeness. In recent years it seemed he had become more and more withdrawn as if nothing in his life warranted talking about.

But now he hurried on—what about the kids? How had they reacted at the sight of the empty house? Had she found it hard to say good-bye? Remember, spring break wasn't too far away, and then they'd see them again.

They reached the baggage carousel, and their conversation switched to more immediate considerations. How many bags did she have? Could she handle them alone, or should he wait to go pick up the car. Okay, he'd get the car and meet her at the curb, there at the north exit. She could watch from inside for him to drive up. That way she wouldn't get wet. And with that, he was gone.

For the first time, Kitty looked outside, and yes, it was wet. Everywhere she looked people were dashing and splashing about half-hidden under colorful umbrellas. Umbrellas? Yes. Something she had rarely carried. Somehow they'd never become popular back home. They went with rain, not snow. Another change she'd have to get used to.

# Chapter 5

The car heater was running, the windows defogged, as Kitty slid into the passenger seat and Phil finished loading her luggage. It wasn't cold with the dry winter bite that she was accustomed to, but the damp, moist air of Oregon seemed bone chilling, none-the-less. "You'll get used to it," Phil assured her as he took his seat beside her, "and the girls at the office maintain Oregon rain has its advantages. The moist air keeps your skin nice and soft, they tell me. None of that dry, itchy, winter-skin like we used to get. Supposedly, the moisture keeps you looking young—eliminates those age lines and wrinkles. At first I thought they were just being defensive when I complained about the rain during my first months on the job. I have to admit I grumbled at first about the damp and gray, but now I'm used to it, I think they may be right. Besides, it's been mighty nice not to have to shovel snow and defrost the car every morning."

Phil changed the subject as they drove out of the city. "How about some dinner? Did they feed you anything on the plane?"

"Dinner? Is it really that time already? Actually I haven't had lunch yet, and yes, I'm hungry. I slept through most of the flight. Madge and I had so much to talk about last night, and though the flight didn't leave until 10:00, it still meant rather an early start to the airport. Oh, Phil, it's going to take some getting used to for me to make this change. It seemed so strange not going to work this morning. And I will miss not having Madge as a neighbor. Incidentally, have you met any of our new neighbors?"

"Only briefly. People tend to stay indoors during the winter. But I'm told folks start planting their gardens here in March instead of June. And we do have a spot for a garden. You know me, still the old farm kid. And they say even tomatoes do well here. How about that! Remember how when we were first married we tried to raise a garden? It will be fun to try again, won't it? And this time maybe we'll get enough back to pay for the seed."

Garden? That had been such a long time ago, but Phil sounded so enthusiastic. Perhaps she, too, could get into that once more, and wasn't Portland supposed to be the rose capital of the world? She had always enjoyed roses. Would they do equally well in Corvallis?

"Speaking of gardens, is there any place around here that serves up some of those veggies you're dreaming about? I really am getting hungry. Let's see what we can find."

"Coming right up. There's a cute little Italian place I spotted just down the road. Would that suit you, whether its lunch or dinner you want," Phil replied. A drift of oregano and garlic filled the air, beckoning them in as Papa Luigi, or whatever his name was, opened the restaurant door to usher them in from the rain.

The atmosphere was perfect. Crisp white linen cloths, soft candlelight glowing through amber glass holders at each table, hand painted scenes of old Italy adorning the walls. All the place lacked was a roaming violinist to serenade them, but soft strains of *Vilia*, or... was it *Back to Sorento*, wafted from the stereo as a good substitute. Very romantic, and she could do with a little romance just now.

* * * *

Night had fallen by the time they left the restaurant. What a charming place Phil had spotted for their first dinner together after the long separation—romantic atmosphere, excellent food. Following a delicious meal with an extravagant crème brûlée dessert, they had lingered on, sipping the last of the wine they ordered. In this environment, away from the pressures of the last months, Kitty found herself warming to the changes the move was bringing as they recalled memories of their early years of marriage. That same feeling of anticipation she had known when they first launched their lives into an unknown future began to emerge. Those were happy years, each of them fearlessly anticipating whatever lay ahead. For a long time all had gone well. Phil was enthusiastic about his teaching and the research he was doing as a professor at the university. Year by year, he moved ahead gaining recognition in his field. Content with her newfound domesticity, she enjoyed the role of homemaker, wife and mother. Willingly she put aside her own career hopes of becoming a journalist. There'd be time for that later, she told herself. Then, with the children grown, she'd left the nest and gone back to work. It was time to reach out, pursue her own dreams, they agreed. And she had found the perfect job with the new start-up publication *Maine Scene* magazine.

All seemed to be going well until two years ago. That was when Phil started getting restless. Month by month he became less and less enchanted with the career path he was following. "I'm stagnating, not going anyplace," he complained. Then Dr. Lyons, the Department Head, announced he would be leaving. He'd accepted a position at Cornell, and for a time Phil's hopes soared. It appeared he was slated to be Dr. Lyon's replacement. "Looks like I'm finally on the move," he confided to Kitty, "but don't say anything to anyone yet." Two weeks later Professor Benson appeared on the scene, and suddenly, Phil was out, "Passed over, for a newcomer!" Depression set in, and after that the days simply dragged by. He still went to the campus every day, but there was none of the joy, the excitement he'd previously found watching his students mature intellectually.

At the same time Kitty's life was opening up. It was a thrill to be out in the work world again. But at home the close relationship she and Phil had known started slipping away.

Is it that I'm becoming too involved with my job, too absorbed in myself—not giving Phil the attention he deserves, she wondered. Or is Phil just spoiled, wanting to be the center of attention, a little jealous of the new turn my life is taking? What is it?

Then the thunderbolt hit. A new glow, a new burst of enthusiasm lit Phil's countenance. A new job possibility was in the offing. Glad to see the change in his mood, glad to have her former husband back she listened as he described the opportunity. She encouraged his interest, but... She blanched even now as she recalled the shock it had been when he unexpectedly announced he had accepted the position. Still a little stunned by the turn her life was taking she shook her head in amazement. And look where that had brought them now.

Phil's voice, filled with enthusiasm and hope, interrupted her thoughts. How good it was to hear that tone again. Already her own spirits lifted. What if she had given up her own career opportunity? Not that she could ever be the self-sacrificing, non-opinionated, totally dependent appendage to a husband that most women used to be—like Phil's mother had been. She was too much her own person for that. But she would do her best to encourage and help Phil achieve the success he so yearned for. Together they'd make this new life work.

"I'm sorry it will be dark when you get your first look at our home."

"Tell me about it. The pictures you sent were nice, but without the furniture or anything it looked quite bare and foreboding. Are you feeling more settled now since the furniture arrived? Do our old things fit?"

"To tell the truth, I haven't had time to do much settling in. After all, the movers arrived less than a week ago. Before that, after getting possession of the house I basically camped out with nothing but an air mattress, a borrowed card table and one chair. I'm afraid most of the furniture is right where the movers parked it—boxes still in the middle of the floor. You know, I was never much good at arranging things. You're the one with the decorating talent, so feel free to move things about to your heart's desire."

"Oh, Phil, I can hardly wait now that I'm here. It was so hard deciding what to bring and what to get rid of. I almost discarded that old green couch. It's showing the strain of having raised two kids, and I'm really sick of it. But tell me about the neighborhood. What's it like?"

"You'll just have to wait and see. It's not too much further now." Gently reaching to touch Kitty's hand he added, "It's good to have you here, at last. You can't begin to guess how much I've missed you and the kids. It seemed so strange to be all by myself. Do you suppose we can get the place in order before they come for spring break? I want you all to fall as much in love with Oregon as I have."

Kitty snuggled a little closer, at least as close as the middle console would permit. She tenderly placed a hand on his thigh, glad to feel him at her side, glad to be here, glad to be together again. Yes, it would be all right.

* * * *

Mellow with wine and the lingering romantic atmosphere of the restaurant, Kitty watched as Phil slid one of her favorite CD's into the dashboard console. Content for the moment just to lean back and listen to the music, Kitty rested her head against the seat, shrugged her shoulders and relaxed. She wasn't aware of falling asleep, but the next thing she knew Phil was gently shaking her arm as it lay resting against his leg. "Time to wake up, Kitten, we're almost there."

"There? You mean I've been asleep again? Lordy, I must have been more tired than I realized. How long have I been asleep?"

"Not long, but you were really sawing them off," Phil teased.

"What do you mean, sawing them off?" Kitty, roused from the fog of dreams, indignantly retorted. "You know I don't snore."

"I know. I was only teasing. Just around that next bend is your new home."

Instantly, Kitty was wide-awake. Rain was still falling, but through the mist the street lights glowed. Sheltering shade trees overhung comfortable ranch style houses, the style built back in the sixties. "I thought you said we were in a new neighborhood, that the house was all fresh and modern? This looks more like where I grew up."

"I know, but just wait. We're not quite there yet." Phil turned the car onto a curving side street. "This area used to be a little neighborhood park until a couple of years ago when a developer somehow managed to acquire the site. What do you think?"

Through the rain-spattered window, Kitty carefully studied the site. None of the houses were exactly alike, but it was apparent all had been built about the same time, likely by the same developer. Most were two story homes placed on deep sloping lots. From where she sat, the street seemed slightly barren. It lacked the trees of the area they'd just passed through, but the yards were nicely landscaped, and no doubt in time there would be shade trees to soften the new starkness.

"Just wait 'til you see our place." Phil, sounding a bit anxious, yet enthusiastic and obviously pleased with his choice, spoke as he drove on around a final curve. The car stopped, and Kitty gasped in amazement.

"But I thought you said the house was all new and modern."

"It is."

Half-afraid to look, Phil turned to see the expression on Kitty's face. What had she been expecting? And then it dawned on him, "Oh, when I said modern, you thought I meant all modern-modern—the sort that gleams with stainless steel, concrete, all white and contemporary. I'm sorry, but you and I both know that's not us. When I said modern I meant modern as in new furnace, plumbing with plastic pipe that won't rust out, that kind of modern."

Their house stood nestled in a small grove of newly planted trees, and yes, it was apparently new, yet traditional in styling—reminiscent of a New England Cape Cod. The lines of the house were simple, a plain rectangle with a long, wooden-railed porch leading from the walkway to the entry door. To the left of the porch a somewhat narrower, enclosed breezeway connected the side of the house to a two-car garage. The roof was pitched with two dormer windows set to allow light into what appeared to be a second story or attic area. From what she could see in the dark of night, the lot seemed somewhat shallow, but wider than others they passed and certainly there were more trees.

"Well, what do you think?" Phil asked.

Kitty sat quietly, still somewhat dumbstruck. This was so different from what she had expected, but yes, so far so good. She liked the simplicity of what she saw. Now, if the floor plan was as attractive as the outside, well...

"Come on. Don't you want to see inside?"

"Oh, yes." Kitty quickly opened the car door and hopped out onto the pavement.

Grabbing her by the hand Phil hustled her to the front door. "I'll put the car away later. Should I carry you over the threshold, or something, as we start our new life in the West?" He turned the key in the lock.

Kitty smiled and stepped inside.

The entry, though somewhat cramped, led back to a spacious living area at the rear of the house where a long rectangular room overlooked the back yard. The left end of the room appeared to be a dining area. Low floor to ceiling windows opened onto an outdoor patio. The same wall at the other end of the room featured a cozy fireplace set between two tall, slim windows. Phil flipped an outside light switch and Kitty found herself overlooking the patio and a shallow back yard beyond which was a steep, naturally wooded canyon. Trees. Instantly she recognized why this particular house had appealed to Phil. This location fitted perfectly with his environmental mission of preserving green space. Moreover, there wouldn't be too much lawn to mow.

Anxious to see the rest of the house, Kitty turned, and

looking up noted a feature she had originally missed. The high sloping ceiling of the living room was enhanced by an open balcony-like space that overlooked the room. How exciting. Already she could visualize what might be done with that.

"Come on." Phil called. "I want you to see the rest," and he led her into the kitchen where a dividing island separated the cooking area from another small room that faced the back of the lot. Between the rooms a side door led into the breezeway/laundry area that connected the house to the garage. Good. There'd be no more lugging groceries through the weather at this house.

"Oh, Phil, it looks great, even with all the packing boxes and unarranged furniture sitting around." Kitty raced back into the other room to climb the stairs to the balcony area above. Two rooms, separated by a three-quarter bath opened off the balcony. The first room had apparently been used as a hobby, workroom. The other served as an extra bedroom. Bedrooms? This area would do for the kids when they came home, but what about Phil and her? Then she realized that in her rush to see everything, she'd by-passed the room that opened off the front entry. That must be the master bedroom area, and off she dashed to check it out. "How about it?" she called to Phil who again stood admiring the view into the darkened canyon below. "Is there a bedroom big enough for that king-size bed you've always wanted?" Opening the door, which until now had remained closed, she answered her own question. No, they would share their same queen-size bed as usual, but there was a large walk-in closet and a bath, complete with both a tub for her and a shower stall for Phil.

"Oh, Honey, it's wonderful. I was so concerned after I didn't come out when you said you'd found a place, but I love it. You couldn't have found anything to please me more," and joining Phil to admire the view, she wrapped her arms around his waist in a squeeze of loving approval.

With a sigh of relief, Phil returned her embrace, and the

two of them clung to each other in a moment of passion. Finally, they drew apart. Phil smiled as he asked, "Do you suppose that old bed of ours will still hold us as well as it used to? It has felt so empty these last few months without you there beside me. What say we turn in? I have other ideas for tonight before you fall asleep."

# Chapter 6

*K*itty woke early the next morning, surprised to see the alarm clock reading only five-thirty. She'd expected to sleep in, but what was it? Four, no, three hours difference between the East and West coasts? Wake-up time back home. It was still dark, but finding herself wide-awake, she rose and headed for their new kitchen. Surely she could locate the makings for coffee without Phil's help.

Phil's favorite lounge chair was placed by the window in the adjacent family area. There she perched, sipping her coffee as she contemplated the strange assortment of boxes and furniture around her. Where to begin? Would Phil be able to stay home today to help? They hadn't talked of that last night, but this morning she was eager to get started. It was somehow disconcerting to find herself in such a disorganized mess. That stool over there, for instance. Why would anyone ever have thought it belonged in this room? And those boxes —couldn't those movers read? Clearly printed on the side it said master bedroom: bed linens and summer clothes. Cupping her hands around her cup of freshly brewed coffee, she moved into the next room. Well, the dining table was in place, centered under the ceiling light, and the sofa—at least it was in the right end of the room. Phil wasn't kidding when he said he'd hardly touched things after the furniture arrived. Just then he stumbled in from the bedroom.

"My God, do you know what time it is? What are you doing up so early? I expected you to sleep in, at least on your first day here."

"Sorry, did I wake you? Guess it must be the time change.

Anyway I woke up and couldn't go back to sleep. Guess I just had to get moving. Looks to me like there's plenty to be done around here. By the way, will you be able to stay home today to help me at least get the big stuff arranged?"

"Probably, for awhile, but I have a luncheon meeting with the head of the Parks Department at noon. Couldn't most of this wait until the week-end?"

"The week-end? That's two whole days away," Kitty exclaimed. "Oh, well, let's have a bite to eat, and then take a closer look at the situation. I was so eager just to see you and the house last night I didn't even notice what a state of disarray things were in. All those boxes meant for the kitchen sitting in the middle of the living room, bedroom things in the kitchen ... how have you stood it this past week?"

"To tell the truth, I haven't been here much of the time what with getting organized for spring workshops and all the other things I've had to do at work. I've eaten out most of the time. I did get some orange juice and eggs to have when you arrived. And I think there's bread and some jam in the fridge. Do you want me to cook? Or are you ready to resume your job as master chef?"

Resume my job? Kitty cringed at his words. Sure, she was the one who usually did most of the cooking, but was it "her" job? Had he forgotten already, that she, too, had had a job to go to these past five years? Hadn't they agreed then that he would get breakfast while she showered, and she'd clean up while he took his turn in the bath after they ate? Was that all to be a thing of the past now? Not wanting to stir things between them at this early stage of the game, Kitty mildly replied, "You go ahead and dress. I've already made the coffee. Let's see what else I can find out there." She turned and headed for the kitchen.

"Just like old times, isn't it," Phil observed as they finished their scrambled eggs and lingered over a second cup of coffee. "No kids around, new job, new house, new life—just like when we were first married."

"Well," Kitty hesitated. "Sort of, but then we didn't have

quite so much stuff to figure out what to do with, did we? Let me go pull on some jeans while you glance at the paper, then we can go to work. I'd like to at least get these main rooms organized before you have to leave." Putting down her empty mug Kitty headed for the bedroom. Luckily she'd thought to pack a pair of jeans and a sweatshirt in the suitcase she'd brought with her on the plane. From the looks of things, it might be awhile before she located her non-office apparel.

The shower refreshed her. She emerged feeling more optimistic to find Phil already reading labels and trying to maneuver packing boxes into a little semblance of order. Two boxes labeled pots, pans and dishes, already stood in the middle of the kitchen floor, and one marked Julie's bedroom was in his arms. "I'll carry this upstairs, okay? Which room do you want to put Julie in?"

"How about the bigger one? I've been thinking. Maybe that space could also serve as an office-sewing room for me; I think I'd rather share with Julie than with Johnny. She's at least a little neater than he is. Oh, I do hope they can make it out here during their spring break. It seems weird having them clear across the country. What if one of them gets hurt or something? Who's going to be there to look after them?"

"Now, Kitty. We've been over all that before. Remember they're almost twenty-one—old enough to be on their own. We can't keep them in the nest forever." Phil grunted, as he reached the top of the stairs and shoved the heavy box he'd been carrying through the doorway. "Besides, don't forget, this is the age of cell phones and e-mail."

Telephones and e-mail, but that's not the same as being together. He just doesn't get it, Kitty mused.

Phil found Kitty busily checking the insides of the cupboards for cleanliness and mentally arranging what should go where. Mixing area, between the stove and refrigerator. Everyday dishes next to the dishwasher and within easy range of the small breakfast table she intended to place near the window in the family room. She slashed through the sealing tape across the top of one box and began to pull things out.

"Here, what say we work at this together? I'll unload the box and set things on the breakfast bar, and you can put them where you want," Phil suggested as he walked into the room. So they worked. With the kitchen in place, Kitty began to feel more at home, and as the morning wore on things really began to take shape. They argued a bit about where the old green couch should go in the living room, Kitty insisting it should be placed as a divider between dining and living areas, while Phil questioned why she wanted to break up all that open space. Wouldn't it be better placed against the wall? But she had her way, explaining about grouping pieces for conversation rather than lining the walls as if to surround a gymnasium dance floor. By the time Phil had to leave for his luncheon meeting, the place began to look like home.

Opening the pantry door Kitty located a can of soup. Phil must have at least planned to eat here before she arrived. Now, where had she put the can-opener? Ah, yes. That drawer next to the sink. Taking an oversized mug from the cupboard she rinsed it under the faucet, filled it with soup and placed it to warm in the microwave above the stove. Carrying the mug into the dining area, she surveyed the partially arranged living room and began to plan. No doubt about it, that old green couch just had to go. The room definitely called for something light and airy, nothing so dark or weighty. Perhaps she could find two matching chairs to place across from the couch, by the window at the end of the room. She could paint that battered old antique chest they'd bought at a garage sale last summer to sit between the chairs. In her mind the whole room took shape, even to a tall fig tree she'd place in the corner below the balcony to help bring the outdoors in. Outdoors? Only then did she realize she'd not yet really had a good look around the outside of the place. She'd been so intent on getting the inside arranged. She took her empty soup mug to the kitchen, then stepped into the breezeway. Taking Phil's old jacket that hung in the breezeway from its hook by the back door, she wrapped it around her shoulders and stepped outside. The rain had stopped and though the grass was wet, the damp air already felt a bit like spring.

In the daylight, the house looked even more inviting than it had the night before. The soft, driftwood gray of the shingled siding accented by the white, railed porch highlighted the deep cherry-red entry door. Instead of the common, plain cement sidewalk, a flagstone path led across the lawn from the driveway. She quickly moved on around the house, discovering the vegetable garden spot Phil had mentioned hidden behind the garage. French doors opened from the dining room onto a flagstone surfaced back patio. The people who lived here before obviously had found joy and pride in creating this home. Stooping to admire one of the glossy green shrubs that overhung the patio edge, Kitty lifted a leaf and immediately gasped and shuddered as something slimy dropped off and lit on her hand. Automatically, she jumped back, and with a startled fling of her arm tried to rid herself of the creepy creature that clung to her wrist. "E-e-e-k! What is it?" Calmer now, with her other hand she bravely grasped the critter by its back and thrust it from her arm. "Slugs!" She'd seen slugs before, but never anything like this ugly specimen. Repulsed, she shivered in revulsion as she recalled the slimy feel as it clung to her body. Was that what they called a banana slug? Whatever, so much for gardening. If it was going to be like that, the vegetable garden Phil was planning would be strictly his bailiwick.

Completing her tour, Kitty recognized that the confusion and hesitation she'd experienced during the past few weeks had lifted. She liked her new house and found the fresh green look of its grounds refreshing. Yes, maybe this was a right move after all.

* * * *

It was nearing five o'clock when Kitty again glanced at her watch. No wonder she felt tired, exhausted was more like it. But at least a moderate sense of order had been established about the place, so she could begin to really get settled. Who knew when Phil would be returning home? He had a tendency to get involved in what he was doing and never look at a clock. They'd have to eat out tonight. The cupboard was still bare. Suddenly she realized just how tired she was. There'd been a lot more lifting, bending and exertion of physical energy than she'd experienced in quite some time. How about a good soak in a hot tub? That should help.

Submerged to her neck in the healing waters of a fragrant bubble bath, Kitty soaked. As she lay there she smiled to herself as a childhood memory unexpectedly flitted through her mind. What made me think of that just now, she wondered. The bubble bath? Leaning back to rest her head against the tub, Kitty closed her eyes and let those long ago images surface.

How old was she then? Five, four perhaps? She remembered how she'd giggled as she splashed the water in her bath and watched a billow of bubbles float in the room. It was her first experience with bubble bath, and scooping both hands full of foam she'd blown and laughed aloud as a shower of bubbles spread in the air before her. One big bubble landed right on the tip of her nose, another on the beautiful angel fish that was painted just above the water faucet. What a sight that room was. Her mother created and painted a whole undersea mural to decorate the walls. As a child she liked the angelfish best; it was so shimmery and seemed to be swimming with fins like fairy wings. But the bright orange fish she'd named Goldie was special too. Then there was the wavy seaweed, all fresh looking and green that seemed to sway and float above the washbowl. For sure, her mother had both a flair for the artistic and the talent and imagination to bring it off. She always managed to lend her bit of individuality to the shabby places where they lived.

Even as a child, Kitty sometimes wondered why it was their house was so different from her friend's homes. Grandma's house wasn't at all like theirs. Her bathroom had plain white imitation tile with blue or green painted walls, like the pictures in the Little Golden Books Daddy sometimes brought home to her. She was five when she started spending most of her summers at Grandma and Grandpa's house. While she was there, Mama had painted a colorful flower garden with soft green leaves and dainty pink roses, violets and pansies on the wall above her bed at home. Tiny fairies sat balanced on the rose petals, while one beautiful queen hovered above the garden. Mama never seemed to do things like other people did.

I must have acquired my love of decorating from Mother, Kitty thought, but certainly there isn't much else I seem to have inherited from her. Let's face it, my mother was an airhead; no one ever accused me of that. To my way of thinking, mother frittered her life away, always dancing and flirting at that Arthur Murray studio where she and Daddy taught. No one ever accused me of being like that. I wonder— what made me such a studious, serious child? Always overly conscientious and organized, even when I was growing up? Was it because from the time I was only five I felt I had to look after mother?

One thing is certain, though. Mother's and my personalities and style may have differed, but just like her, I do love to play with color and fabrics. Our house in Maine was evidence of that. Nothing pretentious or flamboyant, just warm, cozy comfort. That's my preference. Wasn't that why I was selected for the job of editing the Home and Life section of *Maine Scene*.

Putting her musings aside, she stepped from the tub and began to prepare for the evening ahead. Surely Phil would be home before too long. While she waited, perhaps she could catch the last of the evening news on TV.

\* \* \* \*

"Hi, Honey, I'm home." Phil's call as he entered the room from the garage roused her. How long had she been dozing? The evening news was over, and it was totally dark outside as Phil approached.

"H'mm, what happened to that home cooked dinner I've

been looking forward to. No aroma of roast beef and apple pie to welcome your slave of a husband?"

He was teasing of course, but momentarily it annoyed her. Why couldn't he at least notice all she had done before remarking on what she had not? But that was Phil.

Kitty's voice was a little sharper than intended as she replied, "Old Father Hubbard here left me with an empty cupboard, I fear. So there. Guess who's taking me out for dinner tonight. Incidentally, where have you been? Do you realize it's almost 8 o'clock?" She twisted the watch on her wrist to be sure she'd read it correctly. Her unplanned nap felt good, but now she was awake, hunger pangs were calling as she remarked, "That one can of soup you left for my lunch is getting mighty lonely down in my stomach. Is there someplace nearby where we can eat?"

"Sure, just a few blocks away, there's a neighborhood shopping district. Let me wash up and we'll go."

\* \* \* \*

Emerging from the bathroom a few minutes later, Phil observed, "My land, Kit, did you have to try to do it all in one day? The place looks livable already. Why didn't you wait? I told you I'd help on the week-end."

"Forget it," Kitty responded. "Get your coat on and let's go. It's almost my bedtime." And with that she headed for the door. Wait for the weekend! Didn't he understand by now, that was not her style. She wasn't the procrastinator he was. When there was work to be done, she wanted it done, now.

Food helped, but the annoyance she'd felt towards Phil lingered on. Stop it, she reminded herself. That's just Phil, always late, always procrastinating, putting things off 'til tomorrow, never quite finishing anything he starts until the very last minute. At least not around the house. I wonder how it will go with this new job? He'll likely be setting his own deadlines, but still there'd be a supervisory board to report to. He wouldn't be entirely independent and on his own. She worried a bit about that. It was one of the things that made her hesitant about this move. Oh well, forget about it for now. Kitty's mind drifted off, not really following Phil's conversation. It was good to see him so excited about his new life? What was he saying about an ice storm? Here? In this mild climate?

"So many trees were damaged, and there's concern insects and disease may attack those that were left. It's going to be a busy spring, lots of classes and workshops have to be held to educate both homeowners, tree trimmers, and nursery workers as to how best to control the problems. I hope you won't mind, Kit, if I have to be away from home a lot the next few months."

So that was how it was going to be. Oh well, so be it. She'd manage. Already she could think of a million things she'd like to do to turn this house into their home. She'd have to get busy if she was going to have things ready when the kids came for spring break.

"I understand. It's always that way, when one is getting started on a new job, isn't it? Remember how many nights I worked late or brought work home that first year after I took the job with the magazine. But I hope it won't always have to be like that. From what I've read, there's a lot to be explored about this area, and I'd like for us to be able to see it together. I've heard Portland's a fascinating city, and then there's Mt. Hood, not to mention the beaches and places along the coast. Do you suppose we might be able to do a little camping and beach combing while we're still young enough to hike?" So the conversation sailed along as they began to share and plan.

* * * *

As they left the restaurant, Kitty was pleased to note the variety of shops that made up this neighborhood center in addition to two supermarkets. She'd see if Phil could leave the car for her tomorrow, so she could stock up on the supplies they needed. It was going to be an adjustment getting used to having only one car. No mention had been made as to the availability of public transportation.

"Is it too late to stop and pick up a few groceries, before we head home?" Kitty asked. Yes, she was tired and sleepy, but should Phil have to take the car tomorrow, she really needed to stock up a bit. That half can of soup left from her lunch today just wouldn't do it. "And Phil," she continued, "is there a bus route nearby that you could take to work? If I'm to prepare any of those home-cooked meals you seem to be expecting I'll have to get some groceries."

## Chapter 7

$S$he had the car for the day, but it had meant driving Phil to work. A pickup was supplied for his use throughout the day. Unfortunately, it had to be locked up at night along with all the other city vehicles and was to be used only for work-related activities. So Kitty was up and dressed, ready to go by seven-thirty as Phil gulped the last of his coffee and rushed out the door to join her in the car. As she dropped Phil off at the compound, he pointed to the truck that was his to use, as well as the adjacent office building. He'd take her in to meet the crew and see where he worked another day.

\* \* \* \*

Driving home Kitty made a mental list of all the supplies she'd need to buy that day. Then, as she drove past the shopping center, she decided to stop in at Starbucks. Entering, she was amazed to see how many customers were gathered there, some chatting as they sipped their lattes, and others independently communing with their lap-top computers. This was a different world. There'd never been time for this sort of loitering in her life. Here, the atmosphere seemed relaxed and friendly. It wouldn't be hard to get used to this aspect of being without a job. Cup in hand, Kitty pulled out a chair at the one empty table she spotted and immediately pulled a notepad from her purse. Below the main headings of 'Staples,' 'Dairy,' 'Produce,' etc. she listed the items she needed.

Intent on what she was doing, Kitty barely heard a voice say, "Kate? Kate Bremley. Is that you?"

Bremley? Kitty's maiden name. Glancing up she looked into the eyes of a short, trim, woman, who was staring down at her as if she'd seen a ghost. "Excuse me" the voice continued, "but by any chance is your name Kate Bremley? I've been watching you ever since you came in, and I could swear you're someone I used to know."

Startled by the intrusion, Kitty looked more carefully at this would-be companion. "My maiden name was Bremley, and way back when I was in college my friends used to call me Kate, but..."

"I knew it. It just had to be you. You haven't changed a bit. Well, maybe a little, but even after all these years there's something about you . . . the way you came in and immediately went to work, the way you wet the pencil across your lips. Don't you recognize me? From Denton Hall. My God, I'll bet you haven't gained a pound in thirty years."

As Kate scrutinized this talkative woman, a glimpse of memory began to emerge. Angela... Was that it? No, Andrea, Andrea Hensley. Only the Andrea she remembered was a striking red head with shoulder length hair, and this person was middle-aged with short cut, rapidly graying hair. Could it be? Yes, they'd lived in the same four-person suite their first year of college, back when roommates were assigned, and they'd felt lucky to have drawn each other. You never knew how it might work out, but their foursome had been a good fit. Then in Kitty's sophomore year, Andrea decided to pledge, left the dorm for a sorority, and they gradually lost track of each other. But that was back East. If this was Andrea, what was she doing way out here in Oregon, and in a Starbucks at this time of day?

Without asking permission, Andrea perched on the edge of the vacant chair at Kitty's table. In unison they both exclaimed, "What are you doing here?" They laughed together.

Andrea smiled. "You first."

Kitty, now Kate, replied. "We just moved here. In fact I just got here two days ago. My husband's the new tree man for the area..."

With a startled look, Andrea interrupted. "He is? What a coincidence. Tom's chair of the urban development department at the University, and for the last two months he's been talking about some new guy the city hired. He's been carrying on ever since that ice-storm about how badly the city needs help. So that new man is your husband. You remember Tom don't you? Remember, he was in the biology class we both took our sophomore year. He hardly noticed me, but I had a crush on him, and finally in my senior year, I snagged him. We married that spring and have been here in Corvallis ever since he finished his graduate work. My God, can you believe it? That's nearly thirty years ago."

Andrea glanced at her watch. "Darn. It's almost 9:30, and I have a dental appointment in twenty minutes. Oh, Kate, what luck to find you after all these years. Do you have a phone? Of course you do. Here, write down your number, and I'll give you a call," and with that she tore half a blank check from her checkbook and thrust it at Kitty to write on.

With Kitty's scribbled phone number in hand, she stood to leave. "I'll call you tomorrow. Gotta' run now." And with that she was off.

\* \* \* \*

For a moment, Kitty sat there stunned. What a talker, but it was fun seeing Andrea again. And what a surprise. How long had it been?

*...Let's see, we graduated in 1970, that's... Hard to believe, hard to believe the whole encounter. I hope she calls. It would be nice to know at least one person in the community. Besides, we got along well way back then, but...*

It was time to get on with the day's activities. Finishing the last of her now cold coffee and completing her shopping list, Kitty headed for the supermarket.

After completing the grocery shopping, she drove toward home. It was raining again. Not the blustery cold she was used to back home, but wet just the same. She turned in at the driveway and eased the car into the garage, thankful for the enclosed breezeway that led to the kitchen. She'd pretty well filled the trunk with groceries. It took more than an hour to unload and put everything away, and by then it was lunchtime. Having skipped breakfast except for the Starbucks coffee, she reached for a can of tuna and made herself a sandwich.

There were still boxes to unpack, and plenty of things to do around the house, but why do it today? It wasn't every day she'd have the car. Why not wait until the weekend when Phil could help? She'd spotted an interesting looking decorator's shop in the shopping area, and had been tempted to stop. Why not spend the afternoon exploring? Yes!

Hadn't Madge urged her to think of this new life as a grand adventure? Well, adventure she would, starting this afternoon. The house could wait. If Phil could live with the mess for awhile, so would she. She recalled her musings of the previous afternoon about her mother and what a serious child she had been. Perhaps it was seeing Andrea. Andrea was always such an outgoing, fun-loving person, and more than once Kitty had envied the carefree attitude with which she approached life—wished she could be more like that instead of the practical, dependable, conscientious person she was. Did people ever really change? Was her past too ingrained? Could she possibly make not only a new life for herself but a new person as well? It was tempting.

Madge... She hadn't taken time to call her since they'd said good-bye at the airport and thinking of her now, she realized how much she missed her. There was so much she'd like to share. She could hardly wait to tell her about the house, how excited Phil seemed with his new job—about meeting Andrea. Swallowing the last of her sandwich and milk, she reached for her cell phone. It would be late afternoon back there, time for Madge to be home.

"Madge, it's Kitty. I'm so glad to catch you." Then she waited as Madge eagerly interrupted. They visited for twenty minutes, each anxious to share with the other. "Yes," Kitty assured her, all was going well so far. She'd had a good flight.

It was good to be back with Phil. She loved the house he'd chosen for them, and already she'd met an old friend. "Oh, Madge, you must plan to come for a visit this summer," she urged. "We've had nothing but rain since I arrived, but Phil tells me the summers are supposed to be nice. It's almost warm and spring-like here already."

Then she remembered the journal Madge had tucked into her bag as they separated at the airport. "Incidentally, I don't think I even thanked you for your parting gift. I'm delighted with the lovely journal you gave me. I haven't had a minute to write in it, but one of these days... already I've been thinking about making this move the great adventure you suggested. And I've also been thinking about my life and what a serious, old stick-in-the mud I can be sometimes— always doing what it seems I should instead of taking time for things I'd like to do. Maybe this is my chance to make some serious changes. What do you think? Do people ever really change?"

Kitty listened carefully as Madge assured her that yes, people can and sometimes do change. "But, Kitty, don't get too carried away. I like you just the way you are," Madge responded."

Well, she'd see... and promising to be in touch again soon, she made sure Madge had her new phone number and ended the call.

Looking out the window, she noticed the rain had stopped. Sun was intermittently breaking through the clouds and crystal droplets from the recent shower sparkled like crystal beads on the waxy leaves of the Camellia bushes. It was too inviting. Without a backward glance, Kitty slipped on her jacket, picked up her purse and headed for the car, ready to go exploring. That old, ugly green sofa was still on her mind as she again recalled the interesting decorator shop she'd noticed last night. That would be her first stop. She'd look at fabric, colors, maybe pick up some ideas. Anyway, it would be fun just to look.

As she drove she began to envision the character she'd

like to achieve for this new home—sunny colors, fresh like spring. Simple, sort of country, yet classic without a lot of frills or bric-a brac that had to be dusted and fussed over. The dining set they had would work just fine, but the living room needed a whole new look. The wooded area behind the house screened that room from view, so they really wouldn't need any draperies, at least not right away. A tint of color on the walls would be nice instead of the stark cool white the former owners used and would give the place a sunny effect even when it was rainy. And an area rug for accent would be perfect in both the dining and living areas. She'd start there—let that set the theme for the rest of the house.

The musical tinkle of a small silver bell attached to the door announced her entry to the shop, and a friendly voice called, "I'll be right with you."

Kitty smiled as an attractive young, blond woman wearing jeans and an Oregon State sweatshirt emerged from the back of the store. "We just received our new delivery of spring fabrics, and I've been unpacking. Want to take a peek? Incidentally, I'm Christine—co-owner of this shop."

"I'm Kate," Kitty replied. "We've just moved to Corvallis, and I'm looking for ideas to fix up my new house, well it's new to me at least. My, what an attractive store you have here. Have you been in business long?"

"Actually, we're new to the neighborhood. We've only been open about a month. That's why our spring fabrics are only now arriving. But we had a similar shop for several years over in Hillsboro. Would you like to look around, or is there something specific I could help you with?"

"Why don't I start by just looking. Incidentally do you carry any furniture or just fabrics and paint?"

"We'll soon be moving some furniture into the back room. In our former store, we handled consignment exchanges for some of our decorating jobs. I help with the design work, and my husband refinishes and tends to the upholstery and other restorations."

"What fun. Sounds like you might be just the sort of

place I'm looking for. I have quite an eclectic collection of furnishings we've moved with us. That's the way I rather like it. I hate homes that look like someone just walked in to a furniture store and bought a set of everything. A house needs the owner's individual touch and personality, don't you think?"

"H-m-m—seems to me we might get along pretty well. At least, I agree with you on that point. Well, take your time, have a look-see. If you want any help, call me. I'll be listening," Christine replied, and returning to the bolts of new fabric she left Kitty to browse and dream.

Kitty? Kate? Why had she introduced herself as Kate? Was it just seeing Andrea again, or might Kate be a better fit for this stage of her life?

\* \* \* \*

Andrea called early Sunday evening. "How about it? Could you do lunch on Wednesday?"

Kitty smiled to herself. So like the Andrea she remembered —blunt, none of the usual introductory small pleasantries, direct to the purpose and point. And Kitty in her usual manner hesitated, taking a moment to consider the situation, then replied, "I don't know why not. Of course, I'll have to make sure Phil won't need the car that day, but I think we can work it out. Where would you like to go?"

"Tell me where you live. Maybe I can pick you up."

"Oh, I wouldn't want to bother you, but should it be close enough, that would be nice. I haven't brought my car out from home yet. The kids are using it until spring break. Anyway, our new address is..." and she rolled off the numbers.

"Great. I thought we might try a new Vegetarian place I've heard about, and your house is on the way. How about I pick you up at twelve-thirty?"

"If you're sure it won't be too much trouble? I'd love it, and besides, that way you can get a peek at the house and maybe help me with some ideas for fixing it up. That's where my focus has been these past few days, now that the boxes are mostly unpacked."

"Terrific. See you then, Wednesday at twelve-thirty," and Andrea hung up.

"What was that all about?" Phil asked as he entered the room. "Who was on the phone?"

"Oh, that was Andrea my old college roommate. Remember, I told you about running into her the other day. She wants me to go to lunch with her on Wednesday. She's going to pick me up. Any objections?"

"Of course not, it's just that I was surprised to hear the phone ring and have it be for you. I forgot you knew anyone here yet."

Well, she did, and if she had her way she'd soon be getting acquainted with a lot of other people. It was taking some getting used to being home alone all day. And Kitty drifted back to the brief conversation she'd just had with Andrea. Did she say Vegetarian? Was Andrea still one of those people—all tofu, wheat germ and protein powder? If I recall correctly, she was a great follower of Adele Davis and every kooky food fad that came along when we were in school. Always seemed ridiculous to me. Sensible person that I am, I just followed the basic four guidelines I learned in 4-H while staying with Gramps and Grandma.

Gramps and Grandma. Summers spent with them in the little town where they lived in Iowa had always been her refuge, the one place where it seemed she lived like everyone else. Grandma was around all day, cooking meals, canning, helping at the church, taking her to the library—and Gramps though he was retired by then, still went out to the farm every morning. Had to check up on Charlie. "Got to make sure he's doing things right," he'd say as he pulled on his old battered farm hat and headed for the pickup. He always managed to get home at mealtime, however. He wasn't about to miss out on Grandma's apple pie. Without fail, the three of them sat down at the table and ate together three times each day.

It was different in her parent's home. So many nights she'd have to eat alone or with the baby sitter, while Mother and Daddy dashed off to the dance studio or some other place. Daddy was gone all day at his primary job and Mama usually skipped lunch. "Have to protect my waistline," she'd say. Living in an apartment, there weren't many other children around to play with, so early on books took their place. She'd pretend all kinds of adventures, like the lives of the characters she read about. When Mama was home, it seemed she was always busy, prettying things up around the house, or painting her fingernails, or curling her hair to go out. But at Grandma's, it was different, more relaxed, and there were other kids in the neighborhood. That was how she happened to be in the 4-H club that summer, and she loved it. Being at Grandma's was like having a real home and family, like the ones she read about.

"Honey," where did you put the chips?" Phil interrupted her musing. "Since we both seem to be at a good quitting place for the day, how'd you like a beer before dinner? Or would you rather open a bottle of wine?"

Kitty sighed, "Wine, I guess." She rose to go check on the pot roast, potatoes and carrots she had steaming in the oven—Phil's favorite meal.

\* \* \* \*

It was twelve-thirty, and Kitty was ready and waiting for Andrea's arrival. She reached down to fluff a pillow on the davenport, checked to be sure Phil hadn't left part of the newspaper scattered about somewhere. She wanted things to look as good as they could when she showed the place to Andrea, wanted her to see the possibilities she envisioned for the rooms. As she made a final check, the doorbell rang. She hadn't heard the car drive up.

"Wow, Kate, it's great. I love the way you can look out over the woods, and the vaulted ceiling with the balcony overlook is neat. Can't you envision all sorts of ways to accent that? I can just see the place all sleek and cool with leather furniture and maybe a leopard or zebra throw hanging over that balcony rail."

Kitty laughed. "Well, I love it, but I'm afraid sleek leather and animal throws aren't exactly my style. I was really apprehensive before I arrived here. Phil picked this place out all by himself. Neat isn't it? When Phil called to say he'd found a house he thought I'd like, I was so involved back home, there was no way I could see my way clear to come, so..."

"You didn't even get a look at the place before he bought it!" Andrea exclaimed. "Are you crazy, girl?"

"I admit, when he described the house as being all modern and new, I feared it might be one of those cold steel and glass models. But that's not his style, either, I guess. Luckily he was referring only to the plumbing, wiring and such when he said modern. We lived in an old turn-of-the century, Victorian fixer-upper back home."

"Wow. Believe me I'd never let Tom make a choice like that for me. My God, we'd probably end up in a place with a great garage and shop area, but a house with some god-awful kitchen and no place to sleep. Well, maybe not quite that bad, but believe me, I'd want to have my say. You must really be a trusting soul, Kate."

"I admit it was kind of a weird thing to do," Kitty acknowledged. "Guess at the time I couldn't really believe I was actually moving. I loved my life where we were. Enough of that now. Are you as hungry as I am? What is it to be? Still vegetarian?"

"Unless you object, I'm on a new diet kick. Have you read about eating according to your individual makeup and blood type?"

"Can't say that I have," Kitty replied, "but I'm sure wherever you choose will have something to satisfy me." With that, she grabbed her raincoat from the closet and they were off.

# Chapter 8

*A*t last, the sun had come out. It was a glorious spring day. Having tidied the kitchen, discarded the old newspaper and taken the garbage and recycling bins to the pickup point, Kitty was ready for the day. She'd been reading the sale ads and considering the possibility of purchasing a new couch. Everything seemed so expensive. For two weeks now, whenever she had the car she'd been visiting furniture stores—had even taken the bus into Portland for a day of shopping last week. What she needed was some sort of coordinated decorating plan, and it all seemed to hinge around her choice of a sofa.

The phone rang. "What are you up to today? I haven't seen or heard from you since we lunched a couple of weeks ago. How are things going?" Andrea again.

"Fine, I've been shopping for a new couch. You know we talked about that at lunch the other day. The only thing is, everything I've seen is either too bulky and oversized or carries a dreadful price tag," Kitty complained.

"Oh well, how about forgetting that for a day. It's so gorgeous out, I can't stay in this house another minute," Andrea exclaimed. "How'd you like to go for a bike ride?"

"Bike ride? Gracious, I haven't ridden a bike for years. We used to do it all the time when the kids were little, but after they grew up and I went back to work, that was one of the activities that fell by the wayside. Besides I don't even have a bike anymore."

"Well, if you're going to live in Corvallis, you'd better get one. This is a bicycle town. Connie left her bike here when

she went off to school after Christmas. How would it be if
I bring it over for you and we go off on a little jaunt? The
change will be good for you."

As usual, Kitty had to think the idea over for a moment,
and then she thought, why not? "How soon would you want
to go?" she asked.

"Can you be ready in an hour? Don't worry about a
helmet. I'll bring that, too. Just pull on a pair of jeans and a
sweatshirt, and I'll be by to pick you up."

"Okay, I guess. It will be good for me to get some exercise.
I'll be ready." With that, the conversation ended, and Kitty
headed for the bedroom to change. "What's happening to
me?" she wondered. How have I come to be so spontaneous?
This isn't at all what I'd planned for the day, but it does sound
like fun. And no one could deny this lovely spring day.

It took a little adjusting to get the seat height just right,
a little experimentation to orient herself to shifting gears,
but they were soon underway. It was obvious Andrea was
a real biker as she led the way along the bike paths to the
open countryside. Kitty valiantly struggled to keep up, and
out of practice as she was, she soon began to feel the strain.
Her legs felt like they were weighted with lead, and that
stupid little racing seat left her longing for a pair of padded
shorts and a bigger saddle. What was she doing? Who did
she think she was to so blithely agree to this outing? Onward
she pedaled. Finally, as she reached the top of another hill,
she stopped. If I go any further I'll never make it home, she
thought.

"Andrea, wait up. Sorry to be a killjoy, but I'm pooped.
Remember I told you I haven't ridden in years. Isn't it about
time we headed home?"

"Oh, sorry. I'm so used to this little jaunt, I forgot. Sure,
we can go back now, or do you think you could make it just
a little further? That way the route we're on forms a loop. If
you can handle another mile or so, we'll still end up right
back where we started. What do you think?"

Not wanting to spoil Andrea's fun, Kitty caught her

breath, "Give me a five minute break, then I think I can make it the rest of the way around. It's great being out like this, but I'm afraid it will be a while before I can again sit on a hard chair. I had no idea I was so out of shape."

"Oh well, you'll get over it, and really, if you're going to live in Corvallis you'll have to start biking. Everybody does it."

Everybody? Kitty questioned that, but maybe... There's more than one way to become a new person. Wait 'til I tell Madge about this adventure. She gulped another swallow from the water bottle Andrea had brought for her. "Guess I'm ready as I'll ever be. Ride on, McDuff," she said, omitting the final words she added to herself, 'You crazy fool. Who do you think you are?'

\* \* \* \*

With Andrea's help, Kitty lifted Connie's bike on to the rack of the car, unstrapped her helmet and handed it to Andrea. "Thanks for the use of the bike ... I think. I'll probably be stiff as a post for the next two weeks. But it was fun." Fun? She was exhausted. Her legs ached and she was sure she waddled like a saddle-sore cowboy as she made her way to the house and dropped into that welcoming recliner chair of Phil's. I must be nuts to have tackled a stunt like that, she thought. Maybe I'd better start looking for a job, right away if I can't find anything better than this to do with my time. With a groan she silently had to admit, it had been good to get out. And it was satisfying to find she could actually still ride all that way. Okay, another experience on her way to this new life.

"Where have you been?" The sound of Phil's voice startled her.

What was he doing home this time of day? She glanced at the clock. Only four o'clock. He never got home before six— more often like seven-thirty or eight. "What are you doing here is more like it." She retorted

"Well, I sort of got caught up at work, so I decided to take the afternoon off. "It was such a beautiful day, and I thought we might get out and do something together for a change. Then you weren't here. Where have you been?" The tone of Phil's voice sounded downright irritated, demanding, almost angry, as if she had no right to leave the house.

Well, she'd show him. She, too, could be irritated. Tired and sore as she was, she quickly flared back. "Why didn't you call? Just because I've been here at home day after day and you don't find it convenient to take the bus to work doesn't mean that's how I expect to spend the rest of my life. Today I had a chance to get out, and get out I did. Sorry if I inconvenienced you. So what did you do when I wasn't here? Take a nap? Or did you find something more constructive to do?"

What had gotten into her? She sounded like a real bitch, even to herself. It wasn't like her to talk back like that, and after all, Phil's question hadn't been that out of line. Wasn't she equally surprised to find him home in the middle of the day? This wasn't like them at all. They never quarreled or fought, at least not over little things like this. But for a moment her fire was up. It was as if a fuse of resentment had been sputtering within for weeks; all it took was a tiny spark to light it. Exhausted as she was at the moment, all she wanted was a long soak in a hot tub, not somebody haranguing her as to what she'd been up to. Who did he think she was? Surely she had a right to a little life of her own. Just because she'd given up her own life to satisfy his wants didn't mean he had the right to expect her to be there in answer to his every beck and call. Pulling herself up from the chair, she stiffly flounced toward the bathroom for a good, long soak.

# Chapter 9

*L*ingering over a second cup of coffee, Kitty turned page after page of the morning paper until she came to the classified ads. She was only subconsciously aware of why until one item jumped out from the page. *Estate Sale.* The address was just a few blocks away. Even without the car she could walk there. Still focused on decorating the house, she quickly skimmed the ad searching for a "like new" sofa, when unexpectedly another item jumped out at her. Included in the array of items was a bicycle. Perhaps, if the price was right...

It had been a week since the bike ride she'd taken with Andrea, and little by little her formerly unused muscles were healing. Now she was recovering from the experience, she had to admit that in spite of the discomfort it had felt good to get out that day. And it was obvious she really did need some form of conditioning. Why not? On impulse she went to the phone and punched Andrea's number. "How would you like to go bargain hunting today?" she asked. As usual Andrea was ready to roll. Housework could wait. An hour later she was knocking at Kitty's door.

"Have you done much garage sale shopping?" Andrea asked, and Kitty admitted that she was a novice, except for the experience she'd had when holding her own sale before moving. "Maybe it's a good thing you're taking me along," Andrea remarked. "There's a knack to bargaining, you know, and as lady-like as you've always been you'd probably just pay the asking price straight out and never even try to bargain. I bet it would even embarrass you to try."

Miffed a little by this remark, Kitty started to counter, then silently recognized that Andrea was right. "Something tells me you read me like a book. At my own sale I really resented it when people tried to get things for less than the marked price. It seemed like they were cheating, trying to take advantage of me. But my friend Janie finally convinced me that was just part of the game—part of the fun of yard sales, and if I wanted to get rid of things, I'd better go along with it. You're right; it does embarrass me."

"Don't worry, you'll catch on. I'm an old hand at this. In fact, several years ago, a friend and I had great fun starting a little enterprise of our own. We'd selectively shop other people's sales, then organize and hold a sale of our own. We developed quite a reputation, and in the meantime got rid of a lot of junk that had accumulated in our own homes. It was great for awhile, but eventually, Tom put his foot down—said he was tired of having to replace the tools he kept hanging over his workbench. Seemed one or two of these got picked up each time we opened the garage for one of our ventures. But it was fun while it lasted, and even though I had to replace a lot of Tom's screw drivers, hammers and other small items that got sold by mistake, we still made a little spending money."

"Oh, Andrea. You are a case. Never a dull moment with you around. Better watch out. One of these days I might get back to writing and you could end up in that novel I've always planned to write."

"Oops—am I that bad? Oh well, it might be interesting to discover how my friend actually sees me. But seriously, do you intend to start writing?"

"Some day, perhaps, but right now I need time just to get the place settled and be ready for Julie and Johnny's visit. And I've promised myself, to stick with it and get some exercise. One of the things I hope to find today is a bicycle. The ad in the paper mentioned a ten-speed. I think I'm about to recover from our last outing and ready to tackle another episode. And you're such an expert, I thought maybe you could tell me if the bike they have in this sale would be a good choice, providing it's still there."

"If that's what you have in mind, we'd best get going. People and dealers line up early for these sales, you know. But trust me, if a bike is what you want we'll have you pedaling in no time."

They walked on, turned the corner, and there was the sale. The house was a modest, early '70s rancher, but the items displayed on the driveway appeared to have been well cared for. The bike was still there. In fact there were two bikes—his and hers.

Andrea nonchalantly wandered over in that direction. "Sit on it," she suggested as Kitty followed in her footsteps. "How does it feel? Is the seat comfortable, or are you still too sore to tell?" she teased. "The height can be adjusted," she assured as she bent down to inspect the chain mechanism and wheels. No bent rims; the braking system looked to be okay. "How much does that tag say they're asking for it?"

Kitty read the figures.

"Not bad, but with luck they might take five or ten dollars less. Especially if you find some other items you're interested in. And thinking of that, how about a second bike for Phil? Suppose he might try riding too? "

Kitty laughed, " Oh, Andrea—you really are something else. Give me a moment to think about the one for Phil. But what about the lady's bike? Is it a good deal, or should I look some more?"

"Frankly my dear, I think you've found a gem, right here. And the price is right. If you want it, best we go over and approach the seller right now. Why don't you let me do the talking?"

"Okay, whatever you say. I know I want a bike—not just for the exercise, but to get around more while we still have only one car to use. And the price fits my budget. I'll look at other stuff while you talk. If you make a good enough deal, I should have enough money to pick up a few other items I'm still hoping to replace."

The two of them wandered on, all the while keeping a watchful eye on the bicycle, but trying not to appear too eager or too set on ownership. Casually, Andrea walked up to the sales helper. "What's the deal on that bike over there? Has it seen much use?" Kitty strained to hear the conversation as all the while she nonchalantly looked over a table of small kitchen items. Ten cents for that cheese slicer, five cents for the slotted spoon—two items she really could use, and those prices sure wouldn't wreck her pocketbook.

"Could I help you?"

Startled, Kitty turned. "At the moment I'm mainly just browsing. We recently moved here, and I keep finding items missing from my kitchen, things I must have left behind."

"So you're new in town. My husband's going on sabbatical for a year, and we're having to put a lot of our household goods in storage. Incidentally, if you've just moved here, are you interested in any furniture? We've a few pieces inside we're hoping to sell. I'd be happy to show them to you if you're interested."

Kitty glanced at Andrea, who appeared to be deep in conversation, no doubt trying to haggle over a price. Not a good time to interrupt, she decided, but she would like to see what was available inside the house. "May I take you up on that in a few minutes. I'd like for my friend to see what you have, and she appears to be busy at the moment. Why don't I pay you now for these two items, and then we can look at the other pieces later. I do have a few furniture items that need to be replaced." She reached in her jacket pocket and took out a dime and a nickel to pay for the slicer and spoon she'd picked up, thanked her again and agreed to catch up with her later.

Shaking her head, Andrea started to walk away from the two bikes. "Just a minute," the seller called after her. "If you're really interested, how about forty dollars for the two of them."

"Thirty-five," Andrea countered.

"No, forty dollars. That's as low as I can possibly go or

my brother will kill me. I'm just a helper here today. It's my brother and his wife who are moving."

Andrea turned. "Could you possibly hold them for a few minutes. I'd like to see what my friend thinks," and without waiting for a reply, Andrea made her way over to Kitty. "I think we have a deal," she began. "How does forty dollars for the two of them sound? It's a good price, and if Phil isn't interested, I'm sure you could advertise and sell the second one. Both bikes are in good condition, and if you bought one new, you'd pay that much or more for one."

Kitty smiled. "Oh Andrea, you are a salesman. I can see where you might have done well with your former enterprise. Okay, if you'll hide the second bike at your house until Father's Day. I'll spring it on Phil as a surprise—a way to see that he takes some time off to play this summer, even if it's only for an early evening turn around the park like we used to resort to years ago." Together they went over to close the deal, then Kitty asked if they might go inside to look at the furniture.

An hour later the two of them strolled down the street, each pushing a bicycle. They needed a wrench to adjust the seat heights before they could ride, and Kitty would return that evening to pick up the other items she'd bought. It had been a fun morning. In addition to the bicycles, she'd found a couple of other surprises—a cute little curio cabinet she knew Julie would love, and a telescope for Johnny. The telescope was a bit of a splurge, but he'd always wanted one, and this one was a real bargain. It would be fun to surprise the kids with these gifts when they arrived.

# Chapter 10

*D*<sup>ear</sup> *Madge,*

*Almost three months since I arrived here. Can you believe it? You told me to think of this as a "grand adventure," and I've tried to remember those words of wisdom. Sometimes it works, sometimes not. Keeping busy helps, and that I have been doing. But you'll never know how many days I long to sit down with you for one of those good heart-to-heart chats we used to have over a cup of that special tea of yours. Since that's not possible, I've decided to write and have my say on paper instead. Don't let the shock of receiving some snail mail throw you. It can still happen.*

*As I said, I do keep busy. I so want to have the house organized and feeling like home when the kids arrive for spring break, that I've really been on a tear. I know their memories are tied to the house where they grew up, the neighbors we had, the community, and this house will never take the place of that for them, but... If only they'll remember that it's family that matters, not our surroundings. And maybe if the place is inviting and comfortable it will still feel a little like home.*

*Anyway, it was a lucky day when I ran into*

Andrea, the former roommate I told you about. She's
been great to help introduce me to the community.
Got me started exploring and bargain hunting as
I've tried to fix up the house. She's big on garage
and estate sales, picks up all kind of bargains, and
I've been going with her. I find many little things
need to be replaced since we had that big garage sale
before I left. It's been kind of fun, especially since
I'm trying to redecorate on a tight budget. The fact
that I'm unemployed does make a difference, in more
ways than one. Anyway, at one of the sales I picked
up an old, but almost unused, ten-speed bike. I'm
still trying to master shifting through all the gears,
but it's nice to have this transportation since Phil
takes the car to work most days. Now the weather
is drier I've even ventured out with Andrea to ride
in the country. That's a change, isn't it! You know
how I always hated exercise, never was an athlete,
but this is good for me. Gets me out of the house and
hopefully will firm up those spots where middle age
spread is beginning to creep.

Phil stays so busy with his job he's hardly ever
home. Lots of evening and Saturday workshops, and
when he does get a Saturday or night off, he's so
exhausted all he wants to do is collapse and devour
the paper. I can't remember when the two of us have
had time for a good, intimate conversation. Seems
it's always just routine day-to-day necessities. I
don't mean to complain, but it's almost as if we
live in the same house but not together. Oh well,
hopefully with time, this too will pass.

Madge, you just have to come for a visit this
summer. I think you'll like what I've done with the

*house. After looking at new davenports I decided the shape of our old green monster wasn't too bad. All the new stuff is so big and bulky, too much for this house, so rather than buy a new couch I decided to have the old one recovered at the cute little decorator shop I told you about, the one I discovered my first week here. The decorator, Christine, worked with me to select fabrics for the couch and two occasional chairs I picked up at an estate sale and now our new living room is gorgeous. We used a beautiful, but practical, linen-look fabric on the couch, in a color that's neutral, but blends with all the cheery, spring colors and prints I like. I chose a pattern for the chairs that picks up those colors. Fortunately, Phil is happy with the result. He wasn't able to participate much in the planning, but I'd bring home samples to show him, and he'd look and grunt "no," or "that's not bad," or "yeah, I like that one." Now if only the kids will like it, too. Andrea offered to help me paint the walls—she seems to need constant activity and people around to fill her days to keep her happy. Different from me, I still need some quiet time for myself. Anyway, we did the walls in a soft, golden-ivory shade that makes it feel like the sun is shining whether it's raining outside or not.*

*In the process of all this decorating I became well acquainted with the shop owners. In fact, Christine asked me if I might consider working for them one day a week, so she could take a day off to catch up at home. I told her I'd think about it. I do miss the outside contacts I found through my old job, and although this wouldn't be the same, it would at least get me out of the house and bring in a little pin*

money. And maybe by working only one day a week,
I could use some of the rest of my time to retry my
hand at free-lance writing.

Phil and I did spend one weekend working
together, planting the vegetable garden he's always
wanted. He seems to find working there and in the
flowerbeds a great form of relaxation. Helps clear
his mind, he says. My thought is that it takes him
back to his youth and all the memories of his days
growing up on that Idaho farm. His folks always had
a huge garden, and his mother canned the produce.
Her cellar was a work of art with all its rows of
peaches, pears, plums, green beans, and pickles, not
to mention jams and jellies. Just so he doesn't get the
idea for me to follow through in that vein.

While I was helping him plant, our next door
neighbors were also out in their yard so came over to
introduce themselves. He's a professor at the college,
and she's a stay-at-home wife, but appears to be
involved in a lot of volunteer work. She mentioned
the symphony board, the art museum, and a poetry
workshop program she attends. When I mentioned
having worked as a magazine columnist she became
quite enthusiastic and offered to help me meet a
friend of hers who's in a local writers' group. The
neighbor, is a woman about your age, Madge, or so
I'm guessing. She has no children at home. Perhaps
we can have them over for wine or supper some
night if Phil ever gets to the place where he comes
home at a decent hour. It's so frustrating trying to
cook for someone who never arrives when expected,
and it seems that, now I'm not employed, the kitchen
is strictly my bailiwick. So much for equal rights and

*freedom from housework.*

*Incidentally, did I tell you about the comment Andrea made the other day that so took me by surprise? She thinks I'm terribly out of step with the times, the way I continue to adapt my life to Phil's. As I've told you she's a free spirit, and a bit of a character. She's also big on women's' rights and 50-50 marriages—even continues to use her maiden name. Looking after her husband's needs is definitely not her primary concern. It's up to him to take care of himself. But it really shocked me when she announced that this even pertains to housework. She makes her side of the bed, and if Tom wants his side made, that's up to him. Is that really what equal rights means?*

*I told you I needed a visit— someone to listen to me prattle, and who else could I turn to? Thanks for being such a good friend. I really miss you.*

*Love always,*
*Kitty*

# Chapter 11

$T$he house was silent, totally without evidence of human presence, as Phil entered from the garage. "Kit, I'm home. Where are you?" he called. She was almost always there to greet him, busy in the kitchen or sitting in his big chair in the family room, the TV on, or engrossed in some book she was reading. But now, nothing, no one. A pile of mail lay on the counter, mostly ads and junk as usual. Shrugging his coat off, he called again. No answer. Baffled by this, he headed for the bedroom preparing to change into work clothes. Perhaps Kitty was off on another of those long bike rides she'd been making lately. Well, if she wasn't home, perhaps he could spend a little time in the garden. Then, as he entered the bedroom, he saw her.

Curled in a tight little ball, Kitty lay on the bed, her hair tousled, her eyes red and swollen. Obviously she'd been crying. Then he noticed the letter crumpled in her fist. Her eyes were open. "Kitten, what is it? Why didn't you answer me?"

Still no response, just a sigh, a choked sob, as she gripped the letter ever more tightly. Phil leaned over to touch her, to take her in his arms. What could be the matter?

"Don't touch me." She turned away, fending off his embrace. "It's all your fault. I told you this would happen. But you're so involved, so busy with your new job, you probably won't even notice," she snapped.

"What are you talking about? What's happened?" Phil reached out to take the letter from her fingers, but instead of releasing it, she grasped it even more tightly. She'd seemed perfectly happy when he left this morning, excitedly going about preparations for the kid's visit. With the house finally settled to her satisfaction, today she planned to start on a cooking binge—wanted everything prepared, the freezer stocked with all the kid's favorite treats before they arrived. So what now?

"They're not coming. I told you this would happen."

"What are you talking about? Who's not coming?" He could guess, but better to know for sure before going any further. "Maybe you'd better let me read this for myself," and Phil again reached for the letter she continued to cling to. "Come on, give it to me."

The letter was from Julie. As usual she had written for the two of them. Johnny seldom got around to writing, called fairly regularly, every couple of weeks or so, but like a lot of guys he left it to his sister to keep in touch. He saw Julie almost every day someplace around the campus, and she kept him informed. Smoothing the pages, Phil began to read.

*Dear Mom and Dad,*

*Just a quick note tonight, I'm busy studying for exams, but something has come up I want you to know about. Maybe I should have called, but I thought it might be easier to spring it on you this way. Remember I told you about meeting Ken Barton a couple of months ago, and that we've been dating off and on ever since? Well, lately we've been dating a little more than off and on; in fact we have become what Johnny calls a campus item. Ken's really a neat guy, and I'm afraid I've really fallen in love with him.*

*For the first time in my life, I can't think of anyone else. Oh, I know, I've had boyfriends, thought I was in love before, but this is different. Ken is wonderful—fun, handsome, intelligent, gentle, sensitive, caring, everything I've ever wanted in a boyfriend, but here's the rub. His folks have a condo on the Florida coast, near Fort Lauderdale, where they spend the winter months, and they have invited me to fly down with Ken to spend spring break with them. I'd love to go—not just to be with Ken, but a lot of our friends will be going to that area, too, and you know how I love sunshine and beaches, snorkeling and swimming. Would you be too disappointed if I waited until school is out in June to come out to see you? I know you've been busy planning and getting things ready for our visit, but, Mom, Dad, I think I'm in love and an opportunity like this doesn't come along every day. What's more, I'm sure Ken feels the same about me as I do about him. Please—what do you say?*

*I know we were supposed to drive your car out so you would have it to use, but now that you're into bicycling, could that wait until June? Or Mom, how about you flying back here for a visit? You could meet Ken that way, and spend some time with Madge and your other old friends.*

*As for Johnny, you know he's been hoping to get an internship appointment for the summer with one of the national science firms. Yesterday, he told me he'd had a letter asking if he would be interested in coming for an interview and the opportunity to explore the Boston area plant during spring break. He hasn't responded yet, but was really excited about the inquiry—said it could be a great opportunity for him. He wanted to talk it over with his major*

*professor and you before making a decision, but if it
should go through, he wouldn't be able to come out
either.*

   *Sorry, if this hurts. I know you've been looking
forward to our coming, but after all, we're almost
twenty-one now, and isn't it time for us to start
making a life of our own? Of course, we'll never be
totally independent; you're both too important in our
lives, but... Please let me hear from you, soon!*

*Love always,
Julie*

Handing the pages back to Kitty, Phil sighed. What could
he say? How could he comfort her? He knew her biggest
concern about the move to Oregon was fear of losing touch
with the kids, and that concerned him too. But as Julie
said, they were almost twenty-one. The apron strings had
to be untied sometime. It had been hard for his own mother
when he left home, but he'd left right out of high school—
gone clear across the country to accept the scholarship
he'd been granted at Dartmouth. And then he'd been called
for military duty. Admittedly, he still thought of the farm
as home though he'd never been back there to stay for any
length of time.

Kitty, he knew, never felt she really had a stable spot
to call home while she was growing up after her parent's
divorce. Life with her grandparents had been good, but there
was always the underlying doubt as to how permanent that
might be. After all, her grandparents were getting older, and
who knew but what her father might decide to take her back
to live with him and his new wife. As a result, from the start,
she had been adamant about the importance of making their
home and lives perfect for the twins. Every child needs that
foundation, she maintained. And it had been almost perfect,
Phil had to admit, until he stirred things up questioning the

work he was doing at the university, resenting the way he was being treated in the department. Then, when he was passed up for promotion—that had done it. He'd been offered other jobs, other opportunities before, but this time he'd made up his mind. He knew Kitty was reluctant to change, but at his stage of life there wouldn't be many other chances, and for his own self respect, it was time to make a move. Until today, Kitty seemed to be adapting, going along with the move, but what had she really been thinking, feeling?

Again, Phil knelt to take Kitty in his arms. Again, she pushed him away. "Come on, Kitten. I'm sorry. You go in and wash your face, and I'll go fix us some supper. How does an omelet sound? We'll see if I still have the touch for making one of those things—and a salad. How'd it be if I opened a special bottle of wine? Do we have any French bread in the freezer?"

No answer. "Come on Kit. It's not doing either of us any good for you to just lie there like that. Go on, wash up, and after we've eaten we can talk. How does that sound?"

Still, Kitty just lay there; then quietly she whispered, "You go ahead. I don't want anything to eat. Just leave me alone."

What had gotten into her? What was he supposed to do? Totally baffled with this turn of events, Phil did as she asked, and headed for the kitchen. Maybe when the food was ready she'd relent and come join him. First to the freezer to look for the bread. In the fridge he found two kinds of cheese to add to the omelet, a couple of green onions, and luckily, plenty of ingredients for his specialty salad. He went to work, even as his mind dwelt elsewhere. He could understand her disappointment, but why was she taking it out on him?

When the meal was ready, he again went in to call her. Still no response, she just lay there. Was she really asleep, or just pretending? Either way, maybe it was best to leave her alone, let her work this out on her own. Quietly, he picked up the afghan they kept across the foot of the bed and gently covered her. Returning to the kitchen, he put some music on the stereo and alone, sat down to eat.

Bedtime came, and still no Kitty. Once he thought he heard her in the bathroom, but he couldn't be sure. When he finally went to bed, sure enough she'd been up, changed into pajamas, and was sound asleep beneath the covers. Silently he undressed, brushed his teeth, and trying not to disturb her, crawled in beside her.

This wasn't like Kitty, at all. She was always so affable, so considerate, so understanding. Why this sudden change? Surely it had to do with that letter from Julie, but was she just disappointed at the thought of the kids not coming, or was it more than that? Was it such a surprise that Julie thought she was in love? Or was she worried that with Johnny considering an internship in the East, they might be losing him for good? Personally, he was downright proud of the boy—only a junior and already looking ahead, thinking about a future career. Well, until she was ready to talk, there was nothing more he could do. Instead of reaching out to cuddle like two spoons as they usually did, Phil turned his back to hers, disgustedly thumped his pillow into position, and tried to go to sleep.

Seven A.M. The alarm clock rang at its usual time. Damn, he'd meant to turn the darned thing off last night. This was Saturday, their day to catch a few extra winks of sleep. Besides, he'd had a restless night, seemed like only a few minutes ago when he finally fell into a sound sleep. And Kitty? Phil turned to check her side of the bed. Empty, and then he heard the shower running. Good; at least she was up. Pushing the covers away, he swung his feet to the floor and dragged himself to the bathroom. The shower was still running, the room full of steam. Kitty never thought to turn on the fan before stepping into the shower. He turned it on, and over the roar of the fan offered his usual, "Morning, Kitten." No response. Didn't she hear him? Oh, well. He turned on the cold water and splashed his face and hair in an effort to jolt himself wide-awake.

The shower door slid open and Kitty stepped out. "Hand me that towel over there, will you?"

No good morning, no please, just hand me the towel. They rarely spat at each other like that so why this cold shoulder now? He didn't get it. But if that was the way she wanted it, okay he'd go along, for now. He handed her the towel and went back to scrubbing the sleep from his eyes as she dried herself, reached for the after shower lotion she always used, then walked into the bedroom to dress. Without comment, he stepped into the shower, shaved, and when he entered the bedroom, Kitty was gone. The sound of the coffee grinder assured him she was in her usual place starting breakfast. Good, maybe things would be all right after all.

This being Saturday, instead of his usual slacks, Phil pulled on jeans and a sweatshirt. He really should go into the office for a little while today, but he'd see. Kitty had made several remarks about the long hours he'd been putting in on the job. Could that be part of the problem? Maybe he'd just take it easy today—catch up somehow next week. Besides there was plenty of weeding and work to be done in the garden.

*Oh what a beautiful Morning.* Phil whistled the tune as he swept into the kitchen with a cheery greeting. "Feeling better, Kitten? Did you get a good night's sleep?"

Silence. Enough was enough. Disgusted, his ire up, Phil demanded, "Okay, Kitty. What's going on? Why the silence? It's not doing either of us any good. If you're angry with me about something, say so. The least you can do is get it out in the open, so I can be sure what's bothering you." He waited, then taking her by the shoulders, he turned her so she had to face him as he forcibly demanded, "Come on—out with it. What's got into you?"

Kitty's lips quivered, as trying to control her emotions, she whimpered, "Everything."

"Everything? What does that mean?" Phil shot back.

\* \* \* \*

Kitty turned from the sink where she had been standing. The sound of Phil's voice, his cheerful greeting! Didn't he care? Didn't he realize what this meant to her, how important it was that the kids come to visit their new home? No, she was not feeling better! Emotional hurts still throbbed within, her stomach felt tied in knots. She took a deep breath trying to regain control of herself, but suddenly, a flood of words exploded from her lips and a torrent of resentments rolled forth.

"I've tried so hard to make the best of this move, to go along, be a good wife, support you in your job. I gave up my own career, threw myself into decorating the house, determined to turn this place into a home, our home, a *family* home, one where life would go on as it always has, but I've had it. All you do is work, while I sit here at home, or try to keep myself too busy to notice that we never do anything together anymore. How long has it been since you took a day off? Why haven't we even gotten away for a day to visit the Oregon coast or any of the other attractions around here? Thank heavens I've at least had Andrea to help introduce me to the community. And then yesterday that letter from Julie arrived, and it was just—just one thing too much. I can't take it anymore. I told you when you wanted to make this move that it wouldn't work—for the kids anyway. To them, this isn't their home—no friends, nothing to come out here for. And now, Julie has this new boyfriend and thinks she's fallen in love, and we haven't even met him. We don't know anything about him, and already she wants to go home with him instead of coming to see us."

There, she'd said it. All the things that had been festering inside continued to churn—all the little resentments she'd pretended to ignore, the way Phil seemed to take her for granted, seemed to think she'd always be there to serve him. As If she had nothing better to do but fix his meals and wait for him to show up at his convenience, no matter what time that was. As if she didn't deserve any kind of a life of her own.

"Whoa, hold it a minute," Phil cut in. "If life here has really been that bad, why haven't you said anything before? I know I've been busy, spent too many hours at work, but I thought you understood. Remember, the city's been without someone to fill this job for two years. There's a lot to catch up on right now. But it won't always be like that, I promise."

"So you say," and once more Kitty burst into a flood of tears.

At least, this time she didn't push him away as Phil reached out and pulled her into his arms. He stroked her hair, gentling, gentling, trying to calm her, make the trouble go away, as tears soaked his chest. Finally, the sobs began to diminish, and placing one finger under her chin, just as he used to do with Julie when she came to him with some "Owie" for him to make better, he tipped Kitty's head back, forcing her eyes to look into his. He handed her the clean handkerchief from his pocket, and soothed, "Come on now. Dry those tears, and let's have something to eat. We can talk more after we've eaten. After all you didn't have any supper last night. Things always look better when one's stomach is full. Besides have you noticed what a beautiful spring day this is?" And pushing Kitty into a chair at the table, he poured the coffee and proceeded to dish up the scrambled eggs and toast she'd already prepared.

\* \* \* \*

Breakfast over, Phil spoke, "There now, isn't that better? Nothing like breakfast and a good cup of coffee to set the day right." But the day wasn't right, not yet. Again Kitty's lower lip began to tremble. "Come on, grab your cup, and let's go sit on the couch where we can talk."

Reluctantly Kitty followed Phil's lead. She was exhausted. What more was there to talk about? She'd already said more than she intended to say, but for once, she wasn't going to say 'I'm sorry'.

"Is it really as bad as all that?" Phil asked. "Have I really been such a selfish oaf?"

Chin quivering, Kitty spoke, "Oh, I don't know. It's just—I feel so alone. It's as if my whole world has turned upside down. Just like when I was kid, and came home from school that night when Daddy was packing his suitcase, and mother tried to explain that he wouldn't be living with us anymore. He'd taken a different job in another town and wouldn't be going to the dance studio with her anymore. And then she moved that sleazy dance instructor into our house, and finally Daddy came to take me away to live with Grandma and Gramps. Everything changed, and though I liked it there, life was different. Nothing was like it had been at home. They were good to me and I learned a lot from them, but for a long time I felt all mixed up. Maybe I've been screwed up ever since. Spent my whole life living in a dream. I don't know."

What could he say? What should he do? "That isn't true—you may be a little obsessive, always trying to create the perfect home, perfect life for us all, but there's nothing wrong with that. We have had a good life, haven't we?" And again he reached to pull her to him, trying to stroke and comfort the blues away. Tense and stiff she rigidly resisted his touch. Kitty was never like that. Maybe this was more serious than he thought. Finally, totally at a loss as to how to fix it, he suggested, "You're just tired out, and frankly, so am I. Maybe a little more sleep would help us both. Come." He rose, lifted Kitty from her spot on the couch, and proceeded to lead her towards the bedroom.

"I can't. The dishes aren't done," she complained.

"Forget the dishes! They can wait," he insisted, and arm in arm, side by side, his guiding arm firmly around her waist, they made their way.

As they approached the bed, his hand reached up and began to fumble with the buttons on her blouse. Then gently, as if undressing a sleeping child he removed the blouse, unzipped her jeans, slipped off her shoes and eased her down onto the cool smooth sheets. Without a word, he too, undressed and slid in beside her. Struggling for control, Kitty reached out to him as she murmured, "I love you, Phlip, I really do. What's wrong with me? I just don't get it."

"Sh-h-h, sh-h-h," he whispered, "let it go for now," and he began to stroke her back, trying to soothe the tension away. Slowly she relaxed as his hands gently fondled the rest of her body. He brushed his lips against her cheek, touched her lips, smoothed her hair from where it had fallen over her face. Finally, his hands came to rest around her breasts. Feeling her body tighten in response he lowered his head and gently kissed her throat, the hollow between her breasts. His tongue licked her nipples and he felt them rise and harden. Her back arched and she pressed her body tight against his, searching—searching for release from the tension—searching for him to fill the emptiness, the hollowness that overwhelmed her. Breathlessly she gasped, panted, murmuring, "Now, now. Do it now," and writhing with anticipation she thrust her body into his. "Deeper, deeper," she urged.

She felt the wetness of his ejaculation as simultaneously the overpowering surge of her own orgasm flooded her body, bringing another stream of tears silently rolling down her face. Exhausted, she turned to her side, drew her knees to her chest, curled in fetal position. Spent with emotion Phil spooned himself close against her back, and without a word they both succumbed to a deep, soundless sleep.

It was after noon when Phil awoke. Kitty was still sleeping. Quietly he rose, dressed, went to the kitchen for a cup of coffee, then out to his garden. An hour or so later, he came back to the house to find Kitty, at the sink, cleaning up the breakfast dishes. "Look what I've got," he called, "Our first radishes are ready," and he handed her a bunch of the small, red globes. "What say we feast on a snack of bread and butter with radishes, right now? That was a family treat when I was a kid, a way to celebrate our first produce of the season."

* * * *

Kitty smiled to herself. How like him. As if the turmoil of the past hours was all behind them. But it isn't, not for me at least. Well, if that's the way he wants it, so be it. Avoid, avoid, avoid. No confrontation, no conflict. No discussion, no disagreement.

But I can't let it go that easily. I still have a problem to resolve. And if he doesn't want to be involved, I'll do it on my own. After all, I'll soon be fifty. It's time I grow up, face the realities of life like a mature adult. She reached for the vegetable brush and began to scrub the radishes while Phil set out bread, butter, and plates.

# Chapter 12

"Andrea, it's Kate. What are you doing today? Have any plans?"

"Surprise, I've been thinking about you. In answer to your question, nothing in particular. At the moment I'm in the midst of cleaning the bathroom. You got something better to do?"

"Most anything's better than that job, isn't it? How'd you like to go on an outing?"

"What do you have in mind?"

"Oh, I don't' know—just anything to get me out of the house. Maybe a long bike ride, or a walk in the park? Something to get my blood flowing. How about it?"

"Kitty, what's gotten into you? Haven't you noticed it's raining again? It's coming down like cats and dogs at my house. And you're always avoiding even a few sprinkles."

"I know, but I've decided that if I'm going to live in this climate, I might as well get used to it. Besides, it's a warm rain, even if it is wet."

Andrea, hesitated for a minute. "What's going on, Kate? This isn't like you at all. Is something wrong? I thought you'd be busy getting ready for your kids to come."

"That's just it, they aren't coming, and I just have to get out of this house—go someplace, do something. How about it?"

After a moment's hesitation, Andrea said, "Sounds like you need a friend. Give me time to finish up here. You put on your slicker and rain hat, and I'll meet you at Starbucks in forty-five minutes or so? Would that be soon enough?"

"Sure," Kate replied. "I mainly need someone to talk to, I

guess. See you then—Starbucks in about an hour."

Kitty hung up the phone and looked out the window. Yes, it was raining, hard. Oh well, what the heck. She walked to the coat closet to see what she could find in the way of rain gear. That was something she hadn't given much thought to.

That old rain jacket Johnny wore when he went on that Boy Scout trip years ago might do. But had she brought it when they moved? Yes, she remembered thinking it might come in handy sometime in rainy Oregon. But where had she stashed it when she unpacked? Maybe, way in the back of the closet, behind the coats. She shoved all the hanging garments aside and surprise—there it was. It was a little large, but luckily, Johnny wasn't full grown when he'd worn it. It didn't have a hood, but... oh well, what if her hair did get wet. Besides she'd be wearing that helmet. Not perfect, but it would do. She was glad she'd bought that used bicycle. Phil had the car as usual.

She checked her watch as she pulled into the shopping center. Fifteen minutes before Andrea was due to arrive. On the spur of the moment she decided to stop and say hello to Christine. She hadn't forgotten about that job offer, and parking her bike against the side of the building she walked into the store. Fortunately, they didn't seem to be busy at the moment, and as the bell on the door tinkled, Christine emerged.

"Well, hello. What a surprise to see you out in this weather. I hardly recognized you in your raingear."

"Ridiculous, isn't it. I decided I had to get out of the house, and this old jacket of my son's was all I could find that was water-repellant. Anyway, since I was out this way, I thought I'd stop and ask if that job offer you made was still open."

"It is. I planned to call you today. If you're not interested, I think I'd better start looking for someone else. What have you decided?" Christine replied.

What was she doing? She hadn't even seriously talked this over with Phil. But why not? And just like that she found herself asking, "How soon do you want me to start? As I recall we talked about Mondays."

"How about next week then?" Christine answered. "I'm sort of busy, right now, but why don't you drop by tomorrow, and we'll talk about pay and other details. Would that be all right?"

"Fine," Kitty replied. "I'm supposed to be meeting a friend in a few minutes anyway. I'll try to be a little more presentable when you next see me. Otherwise I might lose the job before I'm really hired," she joked. "See you tomorrow," and pulling the strings of her jacket tight around her neck to keep out the rain, she left the shop. Outside again, she strapped on her helmet, brushed the rain from the bicycle seat with the sleeve of her jacket, mounted and headed for Starbucks.

As Kitty finished locking her bike in the rack outside the coffeehouse she turned and there came Andrea—sleek and trim in her purple and white, water shedding, Gortex bicycling suit. Giving a wave she stood by the door and waited for Andrea to wheel up beside her.

"Well, you look a little like a drowned rat, but you're here," Andrea remarked, and with a sheepish grin Kitty admitted she was a little damp around the edges.

Carrying their coffees and a scone to share, the two made their way to a table by the window. "What's up?" Andrea inquired. "I never expected you to show interest in biking on a day like this."

"Neither did I, but I was restless, couldn't seem to settle down to anything, so I thought a little exercise might help. Besides I sort of needed someone to talk to."

"Oh? So tell me about it," Andrea encouraged.

"It's kind of a long story, I'm afraid, but well... I sort of fell into a state of meltdown over the weekend, and, and, ... I really don't know what happened, but all of a sudden life suddenly seemed so...(how to describe it, bleak, unbearable?) pointless I guess is the word. It's as if I don't know who I am or where I'm going anymore."

"Whoa, hold up a bit. What brought this on? Did you say on the phone the kids weren't coming? What's happened?"

Kitty began to unload about how hard she'd worked to have everything ready so the move and the new house would still seem like home, and then... Hurt and disappointment choked her. Her eyes glistened with tears matching the raindrops that splashed on the nearby window, as she blurted out, "It's Julie—she's fallen in love and doesn't want to come—doesn't even care about us—wants to go to Florida with her new boyfriend instead. And Johnny has a chance for the internship he's been hoping for, but to get it he has to stay back there. Everything I've been working towards, all the effort I've made to make this seem like their home, too, everything I've tried to accomplish since I got here seems silly now. Even the telescope and the curio cabinet I bought as a surprise for them seem ridiculous. Who cares? And besides it just keeps raining and raining."

"I'm sorry," Andrea comforted. "But it can't be that bad. How long has it been since you arrived here? Three? Four months?"

Unable to speak, Kitty held up three fingers.

"Well, what did you expect? It always takes awhile to settle in. The kids don't understand how much this meant to you. They won't let you down—not for good anyway. They won't desert you. Try to be patient. After all, can't you remember what it was like when you first fell in love? I know you miss them, but ... even I got a little homesick when we first moved here. And we didn't have kids we'd left behind," she sympathized. Then, as if uncomfortable with this conversation, she abruptly changed the subject. "Hey, look, the sun is breaking through. Things always seem better when the sun comes out. What do you say? Still feel like a bike ride? Come on, finish your coffee. The exercise will do you good. Just what Dr. Andrea orders."

So much for seeking a sympathetic ear. She should have remembered that Andrea was never one for introspective soul searching.

And I haven't even told her about the job I just decided to take. Oh well, that can wait. Chin up. I asked for it. "Sure," she agreed, and picking up her jacket and helmet she added, "Let's go splash a few more puddles. My shoes and jeans can't get much wetter than they already are."

\* \* \* \*

Some days were like that—one interruption after another, city officials dropping by unexpectedly, phone calls, and then the computer system broke down. As if he didn't have enough on his mind to distract him without that. Actually, Phil was far more concerned about Kitty's behavior over the weekend than he cared to let on. He glanced at his watch. He'd quit before five for once—he'd surprise her by getting home early for a change. Maybe that would help cheer her up.

Having parked the car in the garage, Phil reached for the house doorknob. *Strange,* he thought, as he fumbled in his pocket for the key. *That door is never locked except when we're both gone.* Passing through the utility room, he called to Kitty as he entered the kitchen. What was going on? The place was silent as a tomb, no TV news blurting out the day's events, no aroma of cooking in the air. Perhaps Kit was napping again. But no, the bedroom, too, was empty. *So much for surprising her,* he thought, as he headed for the kitchen to find a glass in which to place the bouquet of spring blossoms he'd stopped to buy as a gift on the way home. *Well, no doubt she'd be along soon.* Phil turned on the TV and settled down with the newspaper. Six o'clock, and still no Kitty. Seven—again he rose to look out the window, and there she came, pushing that bike she'd bought a few weeks ago.

Soaked to the skin, lank wet hair streaming down her back and face, Kitty seemed to hardly notice Phil, let alone speak as she stomped her feet, kicked off her shoes, and stepped into the kitchen.

"Kitty, where have you been?" Phil demanded.

"Don't even ask. I don't want to talk about it. Not now. I'm cold, and wet, and tired. All I want at the moment is a hot soak in the tub," and brushing past him she made her way to the bedroom. Awkwardly, Phil followed.

"What is it, Kit? Is there anything I can do?"

"I told you. Just leave me alone," and without another look or word, she pulled off the old, wet jacket and jeans she wore, dropping them in a heap on the bathroom floor, and then turned the faucet and watched the tub and bathroom fill with steam.

Totally perplexed, Phil returned to the kitchen. Not knowing what else to do, he put a kettle of water on to boil. Perhaps a hot cup of tea would help, and hungry now, he began rummaging through the refrigerator to see what he could find to eat. Seeing nothing that appealed, he turned to the pantry, took out a can of chili, opened it, and put it on the stove to heat.

Forty-five minutes later, Kitty emerged, pink and rosy from the bath, bundled now in the big terry robe she loved, a towel wrapped around her hair, her feet stuffed in the old sheep-skin slippers she still refused to discard. Handing her a fresh cup of chamomile tea, Phil asked, "Want to talk now?"

Reluctantly, Kitty began to spill out her tale of woe. "All of a sudden, after finishing my lunch, I started feeling restless, had to get out, away from this house for a change. So I called Andrea and suggested a bike ride. It was raining, of course, so we decided to just meet at Starbucks for coffee and a visit. But then the sun came out, and like a fool, I suggested we chance another shower. So we took off, heading out of town on this old country road Andrea knows about.

Everything was fresh and green and beautiful. The exercise felt good. Then, when we were about three miles out of town, the sun hid behind a cloud and it began to rain. Then it started to hail. We took shelter under the roof of an old shed. After awhile the hail stopped, but the rain kept pouring down. Finally, we decided we'd just have to ride through it, so we headed on down the road. According to Andrea, that road circles around and comes back to town almost where we left from, but I don't know—maybe we took a wrong turn. Anyway, we ended up on a section that was just mud and gravel, no pavement. We kept trying to ride but the road got slicker and stickier, and then my bike skidded, and I fell over, face down, flat in all that muck. Splattered my glasses, bruised my knee and came out looking like I'd participated in one of those mud-pit wrestling matches. But there was nothing to do but go on. Then my good, old garage sale bike blew a tire, and there we were. Andrea suggested that she ride on ahead for help, but I didn't want to be stranded alone. So the two of us started walking and walking, pushing those stupid bikes, hoping someone would come along and pick us up."

Sympathetic though he was, Phil couldn't resist, as a stifled grin spread across his face.

"Don't you dare laugh," Kitty snapped, but even she had to acknowledge the ridiculousness of the image she portrayed, and she, too, made an effort to laugh at herself. But she still hurt. "Anyway, it seemed we walked for miles. By now even Andrea's slick cycling outfit was covered with mud, and the rainwater sliding down its surface filled her shoes like they were buckets. Finally, a couple of kids came slithering along in a beat-up, old pickup. They stopped and offered us a ride in the back of the truck, but we could see they were drunk and smarting off. The cab was full of beer cans, so we lied and said since we were almost home, we'd just keep on walking. And as they left, they hooted and spun their tires to finish plastering us. Anyway, I'm finally home."

Phil couldn't help it. The story of this misadventure was too much to resist. He burst into full-blown laughter, and reluctantly, Kitty with a sheepish smile, retorted, "Oh well—so much for me trying to turn myself into an athlete." Stiff and sore she pushed herself up from the chair where she'd been sitting. "Sorry, but I'm pooped. All I want is to crawl into bed. Thanks for the tea," and without further conversation she shuffled off for dreamland.

# Chapter 13

Watching Kitty limp her way to bed, Phil couldn't help but find it amusing. Kitty, trying to turn herself into an athlete? How ridiculous could she get? Physical activity had never been her thing. She was always more at home with a good book than anything else. What had brought on this sudden burst of activity? And what had become of common sense? She was always so cautious and hesitant about anything new. Oh well, she'd no doubt get over it. And then it occurred to him—was it that he'd been taking the car to work? If that was the problem, why didn't she say something? If Julie insisted on not coming for spring break, maybe it was time for Kit to go back and drive her car out herself. He'd suggest that in the morning.

When morning came, there was no opportunity to talk. By then, Kitty was snuffling and blowing, obviously coming down with a doozy of a head cold, and in no mood for conversation. She dragged herself out to the kitchen long enough to plug in the coffee pot while Phil poured himself a bowl of cold cereal. Then with an "I'm sorry. Can you manage on your own?" she once more blew her nose and headed back to bed.

When Phil returned home that evening, her suffering was still apparent, but she was up and dressed, and had a pot of homemade soup steaming on the stove. "Feeling better?" Phil asked as he sidled up beside her and offered a sympathetic hug.

"Not really. But I do have something to tell you. I got a job today. I've decided to go back to work—part time, but starting next week I'll be employed."

"You what? Where? Why? I thought you were enjoying being home, doing what you liked—playing house as you used to call it? What's the matter? Are you afraid we can't make it on my income alone? If you need more money to run the house why didn't you say so?"

"Oh Phil, it's not that. It's ... I don't know I just feel lost, like I don't know who I am anymore, or who I want to be. Everything's changed, and I do miss not being out with people more, so when Christine again asked if I'd like to work for her one day a week, I said yes."

"Christine? Christine who? Oh yes, the people who fixed the sofa. But why didn't you tell me?"

"Actually, I did. A couple of weeks ago, but you were so involved with your own concerns you hardly seemed interested. I meant to mention it again last night, but then... Anyway what difference does it make? After all, you went ahead and accepted your job here without discussing that with me in advance of signing. And you were making not only a minor job change, but a total one-hundred-eighty-degree switch for all of us."

"But that's different. I'm the breadwinner."

"So that's the way you see it, is it. What about my job at the magazine? Where have you been, Phil? Don't try to tell me that making more money was the only reason you decided to move. What about personal satisfaction, the feeling of accomplishment. Don't you think I deserve to experience a little of that, too? Being a stay-at-home Mom and housewife was fine when the kids were growing up, they needed me, and I loved being there, but now I need something more, something more exciting in my life. Can't you understand? When I got the job at the magazine, it was much more than just getting a job—it was my opportunity to become somebody, to continue the career I gave up when I married, a chance to do something important."

"What do you mean, to do something important?" Phil interrupted. "Can there ever be anything more important than being a good wife and mother? And you have been, you know."

"I know, and I hope to still be one, but that's beside the point. Everything's changed, and it's time for me to change, too—time for something new, time to make something more of my life. And don't try to tell me, the few extra bucks I brought home these past few years hasn't helped with the kids in college and all. But I gave that up to follow you to Oregon." Kitty was on a roll. More of those little pent up feelings she'd hardly been aware of harboring were starting to surface. She was annoyed, angry. Besides, her head hurt, and she ached all over. Darned cold.

Phil lapsed into quiet. Unusually so. Stunned no doubt by the defiant tone of her voice. It wasn't like her to flare up like this ... at least not like she had been doing lately. What did she expect him to say? Her going back to work wasn't the issue. It was just ... why hadn't she said something? Had she really resented it that much when he accepted the opportunity he'd been offered?

He shook his head, and without a word, walked out of the room.

Exhausted by this sudden turn of events, resentment still smoldering, Kitty dropped into the big chair by the window. She'd been so excited as she talked with Christine that afternoon. True, the job would be entirely different from anything she'd done before. But she knew she could handle it, do a good job in fact. And really, it wouldn't be so demanding that it would greatly interfere with their home routine, and it would get her started on the way to building a new life for herself, just as Phil was building one for himself. It might even become a pathway to the grand adventure Madge had told her to seek. Tears stung her eyes. Why had she reacted to Phil like she did? There was no doubt but what she had hurt his feelings, spouting off like she had. Should she go to him now, apologize?

The phone rang, and forcing herself to respond, Kitty swallowed her tears as she answered.

"Hello, Mom? What's going on? Your voice sounds like you've got a horrible cold. Have you been sick or something? Didn't you get my letter?"

"Hi, Honey. Yes we got your letter, and yes, I do have a cold, and I'm afraid you caught me at a bad moment. But it's nice to hear from you. Everything all right?"

"Everything's wonderful, Mom. But why haven't you replied to my letter. I thought you'd at least call. What do you think? Will you mind too much if I don't come home?"

What to say? Yes, she would mind but ... she didn't want to disappoint Julie. "Oh, Honey, I don't know. After all we haven't even met this—what's his name—Ken? Are you sure you know what you're doing?"

There wasn't a moment's hesitation as Julie responded, "Oh Mom, don't be so old fashioned. Sure I'm sure. Ken's the greatest thing that's ever happened to me. Besides, you can't expect me to bring every man I meet home for Dad's and your approval before I decide what's right for me. After all, I'm almost twenty-one, and how old were you when you and Dad met?"

"That was different, and it was a long time before we went traipsing off together. Are you sure his parents are going to be there in Florida?"

"Mom—come out of the dark ages. Yes, they'll be there, but what if they weren't? Why should that make any difference? And no, we're not sleeping together, if that's what's worrying you. Not yet, anyway. Besides, I'm not stupid. I know enough to be careful about such things."

"Julie—don't talk to me like that. I know times are different now, but yes, it does worry me a bit, you being so far away and all. It's just... Oh, Honey I don't want you to get hurt."

"Hurt! You mean you don't trust me. Haven't I always been a good girl, tried to follow the guidelines you and Dad set for both me and Johnny? So I take it you don't want me to go!"

"Julie. Julie, it's just that I want what's best for you, and yes, I am disappointed that you want to go there instead of coming here. I've tried so hard to get the house fixed up and ready for your visit. Even though we've moved, I wanted it to feel like home when you got here. But if you're sure this trip to Florida is what you want, who am I to stand in the way. Here, your Dad just walked into the room. He wants to talk to you," and with that she handed the phone to Phil. She couldn't talk any more without again bursting into tears. This time she'd leave things for Phil to handle. And off she went to wash her face and find another Kleenex.

\* \* \* \*

Quietly, Phil entered the bedroom. Kitty was lying down again, covered up to her chin with her favorite cuddle afghan. Sitting down beside her, Phil gently rubbed her back as he smoothed the hair from her face and with his handkerchief wiped the still moist tears from her cheeks. "You're all done in, aren't you?" he soothed.

"What did you tell her? Is she going to Florida?"

"Yes. Like I've told you before, we have to give the kids a chance to grow up on their own. What was that quotation you used to recite when we first let the kids go off to college? Something about granting them wings."

Calmer now, Kitty completed the lines, *"There are but two things we can give our children. One is roots, the other, wings.* But, sometimes it's so hard, and I guess what I'm afraid of is that maybe by moving, we damaged the roots."

"Come on, Kit. You know that roots mean far more than that. Julie and John will both be coming here in June. Yes, I said she could go to Florida. And although this house, this town, will never be quite the same as the place where they grew up, it's family that counts—that's what really makes a home a home. You'll see. But I haven't told you the rest of what Julie and I talked about. She wants to see you, and suggested that since they won't be driving your car out right away, she thought you might want to fly back, spend some time with her and Johnny, meet this Ken person, have a visit with Madge, and then drive back yourself. As a matter of fact, I'd been thinking of suggesting the same thing. Thought maybe it was because you didn't have a car around that you had suddenly taken such a fancy to bicycling."

Slowly, Kitty turned to face him, "Oh Phil, why didn't I think of that? I feel so foolish, indulging in all this temperamental moaning and feeling sorry for myself these last few days. I'm sorry for all the mean things I said. I don't want to hurt you. Guess I'm not as flexible as you are. It's been hard to give up all that I loved and worked for these past twenty-some years. But I'll be all right. We'll make it here, and I really am happy for you. You seem so pleased with your new job. I know it's given you a new lease on life. And just you wait. You'll be seeing some changes in me too, and not just as a bicyclist." And with that they fell into each other's arms and joined in a long overdue, passionate kiss.

# Chapter 14

$T$he plane circled to swoop low over the countryside as it approached the airport. Kitty leaned forward searching through the window beside her for well-known landmarks she could recognize. Closer, closer they came as the pilot dipped over the city. Nostalgic longing overwhelmed her as she began to spot familiar sights—the Episcopal Cathedral tower, St. Joseph's Hospital, the high school play-field where she'd spent many hours watching Johnny's baseball games and Julie's soccer matches. Then suddenly, they were landing. Madge would be waiting to take her home. Home? Suddenly a moment of terror, gripped her. Home? This wasn't home anymore. Excited though she was at the prospects of being back, back with old friends in familiar surroundings, anxiety overcame her. What if it wasn't all as wonderful as she remembered? Did memories betray reality?

It wasn't a smooth landing. The jolt as the plane's wheels touched down shook her back to the moment, and Kitty began to gather belongings as she prepared to exit the plane. Then, there she was, and Madge was waiting, smiling, reaching out with open arms in her usual warm, familiar greeting.

They drove at once to Madge's house. As they entered, the delicious aroma of home baked goodies and a casserole or soup greeted them. "Set your things in the hall for a moment," Madge suggested, "I have to check the oven. I was so afraid your plane might be late. Knowing what airline food is like these days I wanted dinner to be ready when we got here, so I took a chance and left the stove turned on. Come on in, make yourself at home. You know where the bathroom is, if you're in need."

In an instant Madge was back. "All is well. Nothing's burned. Now let's get you settled. I thought I'd put you in the same room where you spent that last night with me before you left. Is that okay?"

"Fine," Kitty replied, turning from the window where she'd been gazing into the yard of her old house. "Incidentally, have you gotten to know your new neighbors yet? How are they working out?"

"Not really" Madge replied. "They seem to be gone a lot, and you know how it is in the winter-time. No doubt I'll have a chance to see more of them now that it's starting to warm up." And with that the conversation changed. "Here we are. Put your bag over there on that low chest. I've covered it with a blanket, so you needn't be concerned about scratching the finish. Are you tired after that long flight? Would you like to lie down or anything before dinner?"

"Heavens, no. I'm fine. I'll use the bathroom and freshen up a bit, then come out to the kitchen to see what I can do to help." Kitty replied

"No help needed. The table's set. All I have to do is dish up our plates when we want to eat. Maybe you haven't reached that point yet, but I find I like to have things pretty much prepared ahead of time when I'm having guests. I do so little entertaining these days. Sign of aging, I guess."

"Oh, Madge. You mustn't think of me as a guest. It's just me, Kitty. I won't feel free to invite myself to come anymore if I find you fussing over me. It's seeing you that's important, though I'm sure I'll enjoy your cooking. It smells scrumptious."

Kitty entered the kitchen just as Madge was taking a bottle of chilled wine from the refrigerator. "How about a glass of Chardonnay while things are finishing up? Here, why don't you pour, and then we'll go sit in the other room."

As they settled in the two chairs set side by side for

intimate conversation, Madge relaxed. "Now, tell me all about it—your new life, Oregon, the kids. How are things really going? You sounded a little distraught when you called last week. Is everything okay?"

Where to begin? There was so much she wanted to say, so much to share, so much that she felt sure only Madge would understand, help her sort out and make sense of after all the craziness she'd experienced in the last couple of weeks. For a moment Kitty was silent as she tried to organize her thoughts.

"What is it, Kitty?" Madge inquired. "Is something wrong?"

"Not really." Kitty hesitated. "It's just that I'm so mixed up. I've tried to think of this new life as a grand adventure, just like you advised. But these past few weeks I've been feeling sort of lost, like I don't know who I am, what I'm supposed to be, or what I want to do with my life. And after Julie called, it seemed all I wanted to do was pull into my shell and hibernate."

"Why, Kitty. That doesn't sound like you at all. You were always so energetic. Have you seen a doctor? Is there anything physically wrong?"

"No. I'm sure I'm healthy enough. It's just that I'm in kind of a funk all the time."

"A funk?" Madge laughed. "That's a new one on me. What do you mean by a funk? Just down? Sounds like a common case of seasonal depression to me" Madge responded. "Is that Oregon rain getting to you?"

And hearing Madge laugh, Kitty couldn't resist joining her, as she began to tell about that ridiculous day of the bike ride in the mud and rain. In response, just as Phil had done, Madge, too, began to chuckle. "Oh Kitty, that whole incident is so unlike you. It's hard to even imagine you on a bicycle. Whatever led you to try to become a cyclist after all these years?"

"Is it so impossible?" Kitty snipped. "After all, it's not as if I'm ready for the old folk's home and rocking chair quite yet, is it?"

"Oh no, Honey." Madge hastened to smooth ruffled feathers. "No offense intended. It's just such a change. You were always active, but making time for physical exercise and play were never high on your priority list. You were too busy with your books and your job, or chauffeuring kids about to have time for that. You got your exercise chasing after them and keeping that big old house of yours dusted and clean."

They sat silent for a moment, then Madge asked, "You've told me about meeting your old friend, Andrea, but have you reached out, become acquainted with anyone else as yet?"

"Not really, unless you count Christine. Actually I've been focused on getting the house fixed up. That's been fun. You know I always enjoyed prettying up the place. There hasn't been time for much else. I did tell you I agreed to go to work at the decorating shop for Christine didn't I? I was supposed to start last Monday, but when I explained about wanting to come back here to see you and the kids, and drive my car out, she agreed to delay the starting date. I'm looking forward to that." Kitty tipped her glass and finished the last drop of wine. The aroma of the dinner you've been cooking is really whetting my appetite. Shall we eat now?" And with that their conversation ended.

Interesting that Madge had asked about whether she'd been reaching out to meet people, Kitty thought. Was it really that she'd been too busy? Why hadn't she followed up on that backyard conversation with her new neighbor who offered to introduce her to a friend in the writing group? How did one go about getting acquainted and making friends in a new community once the children were no longer at home? In the past there had always been other mothers with similar interests to be found at work, at the kid's soccer games, or P.T.A..

Putting these meandering thoughts aside, Kitty joined Madge at the table. It was her turn now to catch up with what Madge had been up to these past few months. And there she was in for a surprise! "Promise you won't mention this to anyone, not yet at least," Madge hesitated as she spoke. A slight flush of color came to her face. "Actually, I've been dating a bit."

"You what? Dating!"

"Is it really as shocking as that?" Madge queried. "Why? Do you think I'm too old for that sort of thing? After all, I'm only sixty eight?"

"Oh, no," Kitty hurried to cover any misconceptions she may have implied. "It's not that. You just surprised me, that's all. Go on, tell me more."

"Well, it all began last winter, shortly after you left. Do you remember that little gray house down in the next block, the one that's always had all those gorgeous roses along the fence? Anyway, a week or so after you left, feeling I needed a little exercise I started out to walk to the mailbox with some letters. I was walking along saucy as you please when I hit a patch of ice in front of that house. The man who lives there saw me fall and dashed out to see if I was all right. Nothing was broken, but it really jarred me. I'd bumped the side of my head, knocked my glasses catty-wampus, and they'd gouged a gash along my eyebrow. The darned thing was bleeding like a stuck pig. He offered me his handkerchief to hold over it, helped me up, and suggested I come into his house and sit for a minute while he got some ice to put on the cut. And that was what I did. He's a retired pharmacist, so he seemed to know just what needed to be done. Anyway, while I sat there waiting for the thing to quit bleeding we started talking. He and his wife used to live in a big house up on Crestview Hill, but she died two years ago. It wasn't long after that he decided to downsize and moved here. Anyway, as it turned out, the cut was deeper than we at first thought, and when it wouldn't stop bleeding, he loaded me in his car and took me to the emergency room where they stitched me up. See?" Madge turned and lifted her hair to show the slight scar that marked the site of the wound. "He waited to drive me home, then stopped by the next day to check on me. One thing led to another, and we've been seeing each other ever since."

"Madge, I'm delighted for you! Not that you had the accident, but..." and Kitty laughed as she teased, "Now that's what I call falling for someone. Tell me more. What's he like? What's his name? Is he fun to be with? Is this turning into a real romance? As the kids say, are the two of you *an item*? Go on—spill."

A new glow came into Madge's eyes. Kitty could have sworn she became ten years younger as she talked. Obviously, this was becoming more than a casual friendship. Amazing what falling in love can do, whatever one's age, Kitty mused. And so her first evening back in the old neighborhood sped by.

\* \* \* \*

Early spring. There's something about the air, the light, that's different here, Kitty thought as she woke to the aroma of fresh coffee and baking powder biscuits wafting from the kitchen. She stretched, then lay back for a minute or so to luxuriate in the pampering she was receiving from Madge. Before retiring last night, they'd made plans for the rest of her visit. The College the twins attended being only an hour or so away, Madge suggested that she drive Kitty to the hotel where she would stay, and they could meet the twins there for lunch. After a visit among the four of them, Madge would return home leaving Kitty to spend the weekend with Julie and Johnny. "That way you and I will have a little more time together, and it will also give me an opportunity to see the twins before the school year ends," Madge proposed.

"Would you mind? It would be much nicer than having to ride the bus. After the week-end I'd still like to return and spend another day or two here with you," Kitty replied. "There are a couple of other friends I'd like to see while I'm in town, and I want to drop by my old office, see how they're getting along without me. And maybe you can arrange for me to meet this new interest in your life. Paul isn't it?" Kitty smiled to herself as she again recalled the glow that came to Madge's complexion as she shyly revealed what appeared to be far more than a casual friendship. Funny, she'd never thought of Madge in terms of wanting or having an affair. She always seemed so content, happy with herself and life as it was. Just goes to show what a little romance can do, and silently she recited to herself the lines of a favorite poem she had read and memorized shortly after she was left alone.

I must conquer my loneliness
alone,
or I have
nothing
to offer.
Two halves have
little choice
but to
join
and yes,
they do
make a
whole.
but two
wholes,
when they coincide...
that is
beauty.
that is
love.[1]

[1] *How to Survive the Loss of a Love, Melba Colgrove, Ph. D., Harold H. Bloomfield, M.D., & Peter Mc Williams, ©1976, Prelude Press, 8195 Santa Monica Boulevard, Los Angeles, CA 90046, page 17.*

# Chapter 15

The Inn where Kitty had reservations wasn't far from the campus, a place where she and Phil had stayed the year before when they went up for Parents' Weekend. They'd had a lovely time and enjoyed the quaint old English atmosphere of the Inn's dining room, which overlooked a small garden. It was quiet and wouldn't be too busy this time of year. Before retiring, she'd called Julie. They'd agreed to meet at 1:30. Julie's classes would be over by then. Johnny would come with her. He had a 4 o'clock class to attend, but both had the evening free. The next day being Saturday, their time would be hers except for the hours John had to work at the lab.

"Would it be all right if Ken joined us for the evening?" Julie asked. Of course Kitty agreed. She was anxious to meet this new wonder-man who had so won her daughter's fancy. When she'd asked Johnny about him, like most men, he hadn't elaborated—just said he seemed like a nice enough guy. He'd met him, but really didn't know him well, which left Kitty to wonder if he was really expressing his true opinion or just being loyal to his sister.

Kitty and Madge were waiting in the lobby when the twins arrived. Instantly Kitty was on her feet rushing to wrap the two of them in her arms. Oh, how good it was to be with them again. And she continued the long embrace before releasing them for Madge to have her turn at a hug. Julie, bubbly as ever, was full of chatter. Johnny quietly stood by with a big grin on his face before suggesting they go into the dining area. He was starved as usual. Leaving

Kitty to Julie, Johnny gave Madge a little squeeze as he took her by the elbow and led the way to the dining room. Ever since that day he put the baseball through her window, she and he had shared a special relationship.

It was like old times, the four of them being together. However, in this setting, the kids seemed to have grown, not so much physically but in maturity. Johnny impressed them all with his announcement of the research he would be doing during the summer internship, if he got the job. It was obvious he was the student of the two. Julie, meanwhile, kept them laughing with descriptions of all the social events on campus, and of course, her every other sentence seemed to begin with Ken. Then it was Kitty's turn to tell them all about Phil, his job, and the new house that was now home.

"Is Oregon really as rainy as everyone says it is?" Julie, the sun-lover, asked.

Once again Kitty repeated the tale of her biking adventure. "But the sun does shine part of the time," she assured them, "and it really is beautiful there—much warmer than here," Already the Rhododendrons and Azaleas are blooming. The Camellias are gone now, but they were gorgeous," she explained. "And your Dad is having a ball with his vegetable garden. We've already been eating radishes and green onions, not to mention spinach. By the time you come in June it will be time to shell peas for supper," she announced.

Turning to Madge, Johnny asked about their old house? " Does it look the same? What are the people who bought it like?"

Madge replied that she really hadn't had much opportunity to get acquainted as yet. "The whole family seems to be gone most of the time, but when summer comes, and baseball season arrives, perhaps there'll be another little boy to put a baseball through my window," she teased. "But who knows, I really haven't seen any children around. Perhaps they're all inside playing video games. One can never tell these days. But I do miss not having you all over there. You were such good neighbors."

"And so were you," Johnny instantly responded. "Home will never be the same without you next door." Looking up he glanced at the clock on the far wall. "Lordy, it's 3:30 already. I have to run. How about it, can one of you give me a ride to the campus?"

"Come along," Madge offered. "It's time I got on the road, too. Good to see you, Julie. Be sure and come to say good-by before you leave for Oregon this summer. You can have your mother's bed, and Kitty, I'll expect you back Sunday evening."

"Perhaps we, too, should leave," Kitty suggested when they were gone, "give the waiters a chance to set up for dinner. How'd you like to go up to my room? Or would you rather go for a drive or something?"

"Let's just go up and talk," Julie suggested. "I'll bring my overnight case in from the car. I've already checked out of the dorm, so I can spend the whole weekend with you. And, Mom, I can hardly wait for you to meet Ken. He and Johnny plan to meet us here at 6 o'clock. Would it be all right with you if we all went out for pizza at one of the campus hangouts, some place casual where everyone can relax? Would that be okay?"

"Sure, why not. Is what I'm wearing appropriate for such an occasion, or should I put on a pair of jeans like the rest of you?" Kitty asked.

"Well, everyone will be able to tell you're my mother, whatever you wear," Julie responded, "but it's up to you. Jeans are fine if you'd feel younger that way," she added, then handed the tab to Kitty as they prepared to leave.

Would she feel younger? Were the advancing years becoming so apparent?

* * * *

"Come on, Mom. You look fine. The guys will be here any minute, and I told them we'd be downstairs waiting for them."

"Are you sure I look all right? Is this top really okay? Or should I put on my blue one, something a little more conservative?" Dressed in a snug fitting top Julie insisted she borrow, Kitty felt somewhat insecure as she made another turn in front of the mirror. She'd kept her figure, pretty well, but standing beside Julie... Oh well, what did she expect? It was just that she wanted to make a good impression.

"Like I said, you look great. It's not every fifty-year-old mother who can even get into a pair of jeans let alone a top like that. Now, let's go," Julie prodded. With a parting glance in the mirror, Kitty sucked in her tummy, grabbed her cardigan from the bed and followed Julie out the door.

Kitty watched as a sporty new minivan pulled to a stop at the motel entrance. Johnny stepped out, but before he could take a step, Julie, with her mother in tow, dashed out to meet him. "If only all my dates could be that ready to go," Johnny laughed as he grasped Kitty's elbow to help her in the car while Julie excitedly proceeded with introductions.

"I'm pleased to meet you Mrs. Lundstrom. Julie's been so excited about you coming I've hardly been able to get a word in with her these past few days. Nice you could come." Ken politely extended his hand in greeting. "Come on, Julie. How about letting your mother get in the car."

"Thank you, Ken, but why don't you call me Kitty instead of Mrs. Lundstrom." No reason for him to treat her like some ancient dinosaur, even if she felt like it at the moment. How did these kids suddenly become so much younger than she? Or was it the other way around? Somehow the conversation she'd been having with Julie as they talked in the room left her feeling out of step with the times and quite out of touch with the youth of today.

"Julie said she wants to take you to the campus dive for Pizza. Is that okay with you, Kitty, or would you prefer some other place?" Ken asked as he started the car and pulled out of the hotel parking area.

"Pizza sounds great, and it will be fun to get to meet some of your friends. It's been a long time since I spent a Friday night with a bunch of college kids, but I'm sure I can survive." Keep the conversation light she reminded herself;

you want to get to know this new "love" of your daughter's. So far, he seemed to encompass all the qualities Julie had promised. Handsome, polite, obviously wealthy; how else could a college kid afford such a car as they were riding in.

"Did you and Julie have a good visit after I left?" Johnny interjected. "Sorry I had to leave, but maybe you and I can catch up on our own sometime tomorrow. With Julie around I never get to talk," Johnny teased.

With a scowl on her face Julie quickly turned to defend herself. "Just because I'm not an old stick in the mud like you with my head always stuck in a book," she countered.

Kitty smiled to herself. Sparring just like they always had. Perhaps they weren't as grown up as it first seemed.

Friday night and the pizza place was packed as the four of them pushed their way through the crowd at the bar and headed for a table at the back. Over and over again, greetings rang out calling to Julie. It was apparent she regularly frequented this spot as she waved and smiled to all the greeters while Johnny surged ahead scouting for a table. Ken shepherded Kitty through the mass of Friday night celebrants. Luckily, a group of four seated near a rear window stood up to leave just as Johnny passed. He quickly claimed possession of the table even before the waiter could come to clear the clutter. "We're in luck. It's not always easy to find a table here on Friday nights," he remarked as Ken proceeded to seat Kitty. Julie dashed off to greet another couple before rejoining the three of them just as the waiter arrived.

Kitty studied the menu. So many varieties of pizza. "What do you recommend," she asked the others. "What are your favorites?" It seemed Phil always just ordered pepperoni with extra cheese and extra sauce when they went out for pizza, but that seemed pretty mundane with all the choices offered here.

"How about the big deep-dish Chicago style special—it's always good here," Ken suggested. "And what would you like to drink? They have a lot of special brews, if you like beer or ale, Mrs. Lundstrom—Kitty," he corrected himself.

"Why don't you order for me," Kitty suggested. "You and Julie obviously know what's best here, but please, make mine a light beer."

"You guys, go ahead," Johnny joined in. "But if you don't mind I'll just have a small sausage and green pepper pizza and a Bud light. I'm afraid I'm not in to all the exotic stuff."

"Oh Johnny, loosen up for once, be a little daring. You might even like it," Julie deviled her brother.

"How about you, Julie? Do you want to choose all the trimmings as usual?" Ken ignored the brother and sisterly sparring as the waiter approached the table, and in a voice used to taking charge, he stated their order. "Let's see, that will be one small sausage and green pepper pizza, one large family size Chicago Style with" and he nodded at Julie to complete the order ingredients, then resumed ordering "one Bud light and three Corollas. Anybody want anything else, now?" he asked.

"Sounds good to me," Kitty responded, "and this is on me tonight," she hastened to add.

Ignoring her comment completely, Ken nodded to the waiter and indicated he was paying. Then turning to Kitty he explained, "One of these days you'll likely be having plenty of chances to offer a home-cooked meal to me. Has Julie told you I hope to come out to Oregon this summer?"

Kitty turned to Julie and found her beaming with delight. "I thought I'd leave that for Ken to tell you," she explained. "He's applied for a job as a golf instructor at one of the country clubs his Dad has an interest in on the Oregon coast."

"How nice," Kitty responded, as she thought to herself, interesting—what other surprises do these two have in mind? Well, at least that insures that Julie won't object to coming home.

# Chapter 16

*I*t had been a noisy but fun evening. Kitty's head buzzed a bit as she wearily slipped the tight knit top of Julie's she was wearing, over her head and prepared to crawl into bed. Where did that child get all her energy, she wondered. All evening she'd kept up a volley of chatter whenever she wasn't out dancing up a storm with Ken, or some other partner. She watched, admiring her daughter's vivacity and sparkle. The noise was too loud for much in-depth conversation, but she was impressed by Ken's courteous efforts to entertain her. And Johnny had seemed to enjoy himself in his own laid back sort of way.

"Well, what do you think of Ken?" Julie excitedly pressed, "Isn't he wonderful."

A statement, not a question, Kitty noted. How to respond? She hesitated just a moment to organize her thoughts, and Julie, waiting on pins and needles, instantly demanded, "Come on, out with it. Didn't you like him?"

"Of course I liked him." What was there not to like? He was all the things Julie had claimed—handsome, polite, sociable, fun, but ... he seemed so mature, much more so than Julie's other friends. And what about the way he just automatically took charge, ignoring her request for the check, organizing the ordering. Was Julie ready for that sort of thing? Had she learned to think for herself yet? How to stand on her own two feet, or would she always be just a follower letting him take control? And those lovely manners—the attentiveness he'd shown her was nice, but it almost made her feel matronly, like she was somebody's great aunt or grandmother. Where had he learned to behave like that? What was his background? Was his family part of the socially upper-class, elite crowd? And if so, would Julie be happy with such a lifestyle?

She glanced at Julie and smiled. "Yes, Honey, he's wonderful, just as you said. It's just that I'm not used to seeing you with someone so mature. You said he was a senior, but you've never mentioned his age. How old is he?"

"What difference does that make?" Julie demanded. "Sure he's a little older than I am, but he loves me, and I love him, and that's what matters. His Dad has business interests in Europe. Ken took a couple of years off from school to travel there, while his family was living overseas getting their new business operations established. He got to meet a lot of people from the diplomatic core and stuff while he was there. Did I tell you he's majoring in Poly-Sci and hopes to get into Foreign Service work when he graduates? Wouldn't that be exciting!"

Oh dear—what next? Kitty sighed, then doing her best to mirror Julie's enthusiasm she replied, "Wow, I'm impressed. Yes, that's exciting, but I'm afraid you'll have to tell me more tomorrow. I've about had it for today. My head is still pounding from all that noise. It's been a long time since I spent an evening like that. I'm afraid your Dad and I are getting to be a couple of old fogies. Will you forgive me if I head for the shower, then crawl into bed?" As she passed her daughter heading for the bathroom she gave her shoulders a squeeze and whispered, "Oh, honey, it's so good to be with you. I love you."

\* \* \* \*

Sunday morning. The sun was out, trees budding in a mist of green, the kind of day that made one feel glad just to be alive, Johnny thought as he pulled into the restaurant parking lot. It had been nice having his mother's car these past few months, but somehow he'd manage, just as he had before she left it for Julie and him. If I get that summer internship job I'm hoping for, maybe I can accumulate enough money to at least pick up an old clunker to see me through next year, he thought.

Putting the matter of the car aside, he walked into the restaurant to find his mother and sister already seated at a table overlooking the secluded garden area at the rear of the hotel. But the atmosphere at the table was anything but sunny. Giving his Mom a peck on the cheek, he seated himself in the remaining empty chair. "Hi, have a good night's sleep?" he inquired. To which his mother smiled and commented that after yesterday's excitement and the Friday evening out she was so exhausted she'd slept like a log. Julie, on the other hand, did not reply but sat sullenly quiet only acknowledging his presence with a nod.

"Hey, what's going on?" he asked.

"Mother doesn't think I'm mature enough for Ken," Julie pouted.

"That's not what I said, and you know it," Kitty softly scolded. "All I did was suggest that you take things a little slowly. Be sure you know what you're getting into before making any commitments. Go to Florida over your break, get to know Ken's parents and their friends, then we'll see."

"What do you mean we? It's my life, my decision," Julie instantly shot back.

"Come on you two. What's happened?" Johnny, always the peacemaker, tried to intercede.

"Oh, Mom thinks I'm still her little girl—that she can still tell me what to do. She's afraid Ken is too old for me, and she's only seen him twice."

"That's enough now Julie. Let's not spoil the rest of our visit," Kitty pleaded.

"But Mom, sometimes you act more like someone's grandma than my mother. Why can't you think and act like my friend's moms? Why, when Sara took Rob home to her folk's place over the Christmas holidays, they just automatically put them in the same bedroom. Not that that's what I expect or want, but Mom, where have you been these past twenty years? Times have changed. Just because you were brought up by your grandmother doesn't mean you have to act like her. Why even Madge is more with it than you are. For awhile after you went back to work at the magazine I thought you were changing, but no—you're back sitting at home, catering to Dad and trying to hover over us kids long distance. Why don't you go get a life of your own?" Julie burst out, and she threw her napkin on the table, shoved her chair back and stomped out of the restaurant.

"Let her go," Johnny laid a hand over his mother's, "Julie's been a real pill lately. All she thinks and talks about is Ken. What's the matter, didn't you like him?"

"Oh, no. It's not that. He seems like a fine young man, but the more Julie told me about him and his family background, I couldn't help but feel that maybe he was a little more experienced—sophisticated—than she. What do you think? Perhaps I am too protective, but all I meant to do was suggest that she slow down a bit, give their relationship time to grow, make sure she knows what she's getting into before getting too carried away."

"Ken seems like a nice enough guy, Mom. But I know what you mean. Sometimes he's almost too perfect, not like the gang we've grown up with. But maybe that's just part of his preppie background. If all the things Julie has told me about the way he grew up are true, he definitely has come from a different life than the one we lived."

"That's what concerns me," Kitty acknowledged. "But enough about Julie, tell me about yourself. Your Dad and I are really pleased about the way you seem to have settled down, gained a direction in your life. And the internship you've applied for sounds like a great opportunity. It would be fun to have you at home this summer, although I understand and feel what you've planned is best for you. But don't forget, we are counting on your coming to spend at least a few days before you start work."

"I know, and I'm really anxious to come. We'll just have to wait and see what works out. But tell me about Dad. Is he enjoying his new job? It was pretty obvious he was really getting burned out at the university."

Before Kitty could answer, Julie suddenly reappeared at the table. "I called Ken," she announced, "We're going out for coffee. I'll be back in about an hour or so. You don't plan to leave until four do you?"

Kitty nodded in confirmation, and without further adieu Julie turned and left. Fighting for control Kitty managed a faint smile. The last thing she wanted was to fight with Julie.

"It's all right," Johnny comforted. "You know Julie, she's just being a prima donna as usual, always has to build things into some dramatic emotional crisis. She'll calm down and be back to apologize. Sort of proves your point about emotional maturity though, doesn't it? Maybe Ken can straighten her out." Then without waiting for a reply, he added, "Come on, eat up, let's get out of this place. There are things I want to show you. Besides, I'll bet you're ready to reclaim your car. Wait 'til you see it."

"What do you mean? Has something happened to it?"

"Yeah—I cleaned it up inside and out. Even washed it without having to be asked. That's something, isn't it?" Johnny teased, remembering how as a kid he resented having to perform this job every time he asked to use the car when he was in high school. Kitty laughed with him as she patted the gleaming finish on "her" car as Johnny handed over the keys asking, "Do you want to drive?"

"You go ahead. You're the tour director, I'm the tourist."

Sunday morning church bells chimed as they drove through the residential area surrounding the campus, and Johnny asked how her shopping tour with Julie had gone the day before. "Did she find a sexy new bikini like she talked about the night before while we were all at the pizza parlor?"

"She and I had quite a day," Kitty laughed. "A little more my style of entertainment than the night before I fear, and I have to admit your sister has an eye for fashion. One thing for sure, she'll get her share of exposure to that Florida sunshine she's been hoping for. And it was fun for me to browse in some old familiar shops again. But enough about that, what did you think of the movie the four of us saw last night?"

So the two of them visited as they drove, Johnny pointing out all the new additions being added to the campus. Times were booming and changes appeared everywhere. It was a lovely spring day, the new season bursting all about them. Oh, why did this ruckus with Julie have to occur to spoil this, their last day together.

* * * *

As Johnny predicted, when Kitty returned to the hotel, Julie was there, and Ken was with her. Embracing her mother in a warm hug, she murmured, "I'm sorry, Mom." Then, stepping back to include Johnny in the conversation she apologized again. "I don't know what got into me, but Ken and I have talked it over, and he agrees with you, Mom. Neither of us is ready for any long-term commitments, no matter how much we care for each other. But that doesn't mean we won't continue to see each other. And Mom, thanks for understanding about my not coming home for spring break."

"I promise I'll take good care of her, Kitty, and my parents are anxious to have her come for a visit. She's a feisty little thing, but I do love her, and apparently my folks are concerned just as you are. If I go on to graduate school like I plan, it will be awhile before either of us can afford to get too involved." Ken placed an arm around Julie in a gesture of reassurance.

"Thank you, both," Kitty replied as she smiled and reached for Julie's hand giving it a loving, all's forgiven squeeze. "Now let's get on with enjoying the day. Johnny and I have had a lovely tour of the town and campus, but I suppose I'd better get up to the room now and start packing. Have you gathered up your stuff, yet, Julie?"

"Not yet. Thought we could do it together." She and Kitty excused themselves, leaving the two boys to wait in the lobby.

Alone now, with only the two of them in the room, Julie

again apologized for her early morning outburst. "I'm sorry if I hurt your feelings, Mom. It's just that I don't want to risk losing Ken."

"Honey, taking your time, really getting to know each other won't make a difference if your love for each other is as true as you now think it is. Better to go a little slow at the start than to rush into something that is destined to end in a crash," Kitty took her daughter in her arms. "I understand, I really do," she reassured her.

Their packing complete, hand in hand, mother and daughter each pulling a suitcase they walked down the hall to wait for the elevator.

# Chapter 17

*A*lone in her car as she sped along the miles back to Madge's, Kitty mulled over the weekend's events. They were all good kids, and perhaps she had been a little premature in speaking to Julie of her concerns about Ken. She could certainly see what had drawn Julie to him. He was a real charmer. Did she really act like an out-of-date old woman as Julie had charged? Sure, her values were a bit more puritanical than lots of parents today, but she'd observed so many kids get carried away and be hurt in the long run. Is there something wrong with me for being such a throwback to previous generations?

She thought back to her own college years, and all the activism that was going on then. Not that she'd been much a part of that. Not like Andrea and a lot of the others in her dorm. Even if she'd wanted to be involved in all those movements, the Vietnam protests, the civil rights marches, the power struggles for women's rights. She couldn't have found time had she wanted to. She was always too busy working to earn money to put herself through school. And she'd carried extra credits in order to finish as soon as possible. Looking back she realized her time was spent either at the library studying or at her job in the library. That is until her last year after she met Phil. But then they mostly just studied together, he being in the same financial position she was. Besides, all that bra-burning and man-hating stuff never appealed to her. Sure, she wanted and expected to be treated fairly both at work and at home, but hadn't she seen how divisive it could be to expect total independence.

There had to be give and take on both sides. Just look what was happening now in so many families when everyone drifted off in their own separate ways. She still felt the life she'd experienced living with Grandma and Gramps encompassed the common sense attitudes that made for happy, stable family life. And I'm truly grateful for the years I was able to spend at home while the children were little. Nothing could ever replace those times. In that way, guess I am a throwback, she mused.

During their marriage she and Phil had led a simple life, surviving on one income. Unlike a lot of their friends who drove themselves frantic, striving so hard to clutter their lives with material things, there never was time to enjoy them. It seemed these couples were always taking off on some trip or other to escape the fray. But for her and Phil, in all their years together, there'd only been one real vacation—the time he had a conference to attend in California, and Madge offered to have the kids stay with her so Kitty could accompany him. After the conference the two of them had a marvelous time driving the long way home, with stops to visit a few of the national parks and the Anasazi ruins in New Mexico. They were gone for two long, wonderful weeks. But they'd never taken the kids to Disneyland or any of the exotic places some of their friends vacationed. Instead, there had been lots of simple outings, camp-outs, picnics, fishing trips and summer concerts in the park. They'd loved watching the kid's ball games. She'd helped as a room mother and Cub Scout leader, too, something she likely would not have had time for had she been working. Yes, theirs had been a good life.

But what now? Now that the twins were practically grown? She'd thought she had it all figured out when she went back to work five years ago. She'd loved her job, enjoyed being out in the workplace. And yes, she had to admit, being employed outside the home bolstered her self confidence, helped build her ego, and she was proud of the job she'd done. It felt good to rediscover the talent she had for organization and writing. What's more, Phil seemed to respect her for what she was doing, and they both moved easily into new roles when it came to cooking and maintaining the house. The extra income she earned had been nice to have, of course. The kids were still around that first couple of years, and they'd all learned to work together in spite of a few bouts of name-calling and complaints about who wasn't doing his or her fair share. Ah, those were the days.

Kitty glanced at the clock on the dash. Time for the evening news, and putting her musings aside, she flicked on the radio and brought herself back to present day realities.

As Kitty turned the corner onto the street where she used to live, she noticed an unfamiliar car in Madge's driveway. Pulling up beside it, she got out, reached in the back for her overnight bag and went on up to the door. Instead of ringing the bell, she opened her purse, and taking out the key Madge had given her, turned the lock and walked in. "Oh, there you are," Madge's voice called from the living room. "Come on in here. Did you have a nice visit after I left?"

Leaving her bag by the door, Kitty strolled into the room, as a man who appeared to be about Madge's age rose from his chair to greet her. "This is Paul. We've been out for an afternoon drive, and I asked him to stay for dinner with us. I've been anxious for the two of you to meet."

Kitty smiled as she looked at Madge, literally beaming with delight. She raised her eyebrows in a knowing sort of way as she approached Paul, and casually offering her hand responded, "And I've been anxious to meet him. Sounds to me like I'm going to have to share my best friend's attention from now on," she teased. "Madge has told me of how you looked after her when she fell last winter," and she grasped Paul's hand with a touch of approval.

"And wasn't I lucky to have such an attractive lady fall before me," Paul quipped back. "What's more, I think she's been enjoying my company as much as I have hers ever since."

"Oh, come on you two," Madge interrupted. "I knew you'd

get along, but I didn't think you'd start bantering with each other quite so quickly. Anyway, if you don't mind I'll escape so you can talk about me while I finish things up in the kitchen. Better yet, Paul, you'd best come into the kitchen with me. You can carve the roast while we give Kitty a chance to freshen up after her drive."

As usual, Madge's dinner was delicious, the table beautifully set. It was obvious she was trying to impress someone. And the three of them had a most enjoyable evening. They shared a laugh or two as Kitty described her evening out with all the college kids, the noise and music, as well as her attempts to keep up with the country swing dance steps to which she'd been introduced. "Maybe we should try that," Paul suggested, grinning at Madge and asked, "Do you suppose they dance that way down at the senior center?"

It must have been nine-thirty or later when Paul glanced at his watch, pushed his chair back from the table, and announced, "My how time flies when one is having fun. I can't believe it's almost my bedtime, and I'm sure you two still have a lot to talk about. Thanks, Madge, for a nice day, and Kitty, it's been good to meet you. Madge has really looked forward to your visit."

"I'm so glad she invited you to join us tonight" Kitty responded. "She kept you a secret until I arrived the other night, and I've been hoping ever since that we'd get to meet. You two keep on having fun together, and Paul, best you keep the sidewalks clear. I wouldn't want Madge falling for anyone else." Offering her hand in friendship, Kitty said goodbye, then began to clear the table leaving Madge to see Paul to the door alone.

While putting the remains of dinner away and doing dishes, Madge asked to be filled in on all the details of the weekend with the kids and, of course, Julie's boyfriend. "What's he like?" she asked. "Were you as impressed as Julie is?"

"Yes, and no," Kitty admitted. "He seems like a fine young man, but ... oh, I don't' know, maybe I'm just having trouble acknowledging that Julie is growing up. But he seems a lot older and more experienced than she, and I worry about that. I keep wondering if he's really as attracted to her as she is to him, or is he just toying with her affections for now. He comes from such a different background than ours—money, society, country club life, travel, living abroad. What do you think, am I worrying over nothing, making too much of something too soon?" she asked.

"Honey, we all have to live and learn. Maybe you should relax a bit and see what develops. It isn't as if Julie was dashing off to get married or something."

"Married—no that doesn't appear to be in the cards yet, but in this day and age, what difference does that make? That's what scares me. You know as well as I how Julie tends to get carried away with her emotions. And stubborn as she is, nothing I or anyone else has to say will make a difference."

"Maybe that's just as well," Madge interjected. "Perhaps it does make sense for kids to try living together, really get to know each other, find out what married life might be like before they rush into it."

"Madge, I'm shocked. Do you really feel that way? Maybe I'm just an old-fashioned prude like Julie implied." She looked squarely into Madge's eyes to be sure that she'd heard her correctly.

"I don't know, Kitty. Relationships are never easy, and whatever the situation, sometimes people get hurt. But things have a way of working out, and besides, at least when kids just live together, they're less apt to be victims of the financial and legal complications that go along with a divorce." Madge paused, then asked, "Julie does know how to protect herself physically doesn't she, sexually I mean?"

"I'm sure she knows, but knowing and always doing are two different things." An unexpected yawn escaped from Kitty, as she reached to put the last hand-washed goblet away in the cupboard. "Excuse me, but I'm afraid I've had about enough for one day. Is there anything more that needs to be done before we go to bed? If not, I think I'd better turn in." Hanging up the dishtowel, she didn't wait for Madge to reply, before adding, "Thanks, Madge for a lovely evening. I'm happy you have Paul to brighten your life," and she turned, gave Madge a hug and with a shrug of her shoulders, toddled off to bed.

# Chapter 18

*K*itty emerged from the bedroom to find her hostess already dressed in the jacket and slacks she wore while serving as a pink lady. She'd forgotten that Mondays were Madge's volunteer day at the hospital. "I knew you wanted to spend time with your other friends today, so I hope you won't mind if I leave you here on your own," Madge explained. "The hospital called, and they're short of helpers today, so I offered to go in earlier than usual. I hope you won't mind."

"That's fine," Kitty replied. "You go right ahead. I can easily fend for myself. I called Janie and a couple of my book group friends before I left home and promised to get in touch with them while I was here. Janie was going to try to arrange a luncheon date—and you know I want to stop by the office, see the crew there and meet my replacement. What time will you likely be home?" she asked. "Remember, dinner is to be on me tonight. I'd like to take you out to the Wharf for their special lobster feed."

"What a great idea. Thank you, Kitty, I accept. As for when I'll be home—probably about three, but take your time and enjoy seeing your friends."

As soon as Madge left, Kitty rang Janie's office. "It's me. I'm actually back in town like I promised. How about it? Could you possibly get away for a one o'clock lunch date?"

"Let's make it one-thirty." Janie's voice sounded enthusiastic as they agreed on the time and place. "I've already mentioned your coming to Meg and Paula. I'll give them a call, see if we can make it a foursome," she offered.

"O-o-o-ps, I've got a call on the other line. Gotta go—see you at 1:30." Janie ended the conversation.

Carefully groomed and dressed in her conservatively classic travel outfit, Kitty opened the door to the magazine office where she'd worked the past five years. Somehow the place looked different. H-m-m, new paint and a new receptionist. "May I help you?" the petite blond sitting at the front desk asked.

"Hi," Kitty responded. "I'm Kitty Lundstrom. I used to work here until I moved away four months ago. Being back in town, I thought I'd drop by and say hello to some of the staff. Is Ed in?"

"Ed?" the girl looked puzzled. "Oh, you mean Mr. Harper, Senior. I'm sorry, he's been away on leave for nearly three months now, and his son, Mike, is filling in as editor-in-chief while he's away. Would you like to speak to him?"

"Perhaps I should if he's free. Then I'd just like to mosey about and say hello to some of my cronies, if that's all right."

"I'll call Mr. Harper to see if he's available. Won't you have a seat in the meantime."

Kitty moved over to one of the waiting chairs, and picked up a copy of the latest edition of *Maine Scene* she found lying nearby. She'd always liked the play on words of that magazine title. It offered so many options, such a variety of material for inclusion in their coverage. That was what had made her job interesting. Over the years in the *Home and Family Matters* section, for which she was responsible, she'd covered everything from new home trends, to feature stories about interesting families, to unique career opportunities. But this edition appeared to have a different format.

"Mr. Harper will see you now." The receptionist interrupted her observations. "You may go on in."

Kitty walked in to her former publisher/editor's office. At least that room hadn't changed, she thought as she introduced herself and explained her reason for being there. "It's nice to meet you," the young Mr. Harper responded. "Dad often spoke of you. He'll be sorry to have missed you.

As I recall you left the staff to move out West someplace. Is that correct?"

"Yes, I'm living in Oregon now, just back for a visit and had to drop in for a glimpse of the place where I used to spend so many hours. I've missed my work and associations here."

"It's always nice to hear that. Are you employed elsewhere now?"

Kitty admitted to having taken some time off while she tried to get settled in her new home. Then, not wanting to encroach on his time, she asked if she might go back and speak with some of her former workmates.

"Certainly," the new editor responded, "but remember we are a bit rushed at the moment. The monthly publishing deadline is this week. Here," he reached behind his desk to pick up a copy of the previous month's issue. "Perhaps you'll be interested in seeing some of the changes we've recently been incorporating. I don't imagine you've had a chance to find a copy of our magazine in Oregon."

"Why thank you." Kitty acknowledged this gesture as she reached for the glossy covered magazine he held out to her. "It's been nice meeting you. I'll try not to interrupt anyone too much," she offered as she rose from the chair and walked from the once familiar office. Without Ed there, the whole atmosphere of the place seemed to have changed. I wonder what else will be different, she thought as she opened the door to the editorial room with all its little cubicles, and nearly bumped into Marla, who, with hands full of copy sheets, struggled to open the door from the other side.

"Kitty! What are you doing here?" Marla exclaimed. "Here, let me get rid of this paper stuff, so we can have a good chin-wag." She turned to lay the printouts back on her desk. Just then, another familiar face appeared from the corner of the next cubicle.

"Did I hear someone say Kitty?" There emerged big, gruff-looking Al already approaching with arms outstretched in preparation to capture her in his usual teddy-bear hug of greeting. How wonderful it was to be back, Kitty thought, back with familiar faces, and folks who shared a common interest. "Come on." Al took over. "Get rid of that stuff, Marla. Time to gather up the crew and head for the coffee room. What's the occasion, Kitty—just couldn't stay away from us, eh?"

Laughing, warmed by this ready welcome, Kitty began to relax. Maybe things hadn't changed as much as it first appeared. "Okay, everybody," Al called. Stick your heads out and say hello to Kitty, my favorite Home and Family expert." And one by one, chairs turned and wheeled to the cubicle openings to see what All was so excited about. Some of the faces that appeared were familiar, but among them were several newcomers. Besides it was mainly Marla and Al that Kitty had hoped to see. The three of them all started with the magazine in the same year and relied on each other for common support and sympathy as they each learned to find their way through the ins, outs, and perils of what was then a new publishing enterprise.

Brief introductions followed, then the three of them took refuge in a quiet corner where they could privately hash and rehash all that had been going on these past months.

And it seemed there had been a lot going on, especially since Ed had been forced to take some time off after suffering a couple of heart attacks. His son had come home from the big city to take over, and immediately decided to change the whole concept of the magazine his father had started.

"What happened to Lila? Did they let her go after I worked so hard to prepare her to take over that special series she and I worked on all those months after Phil left for Oregon? I noticed it was missing in the issue I glanced at while waiting in the reception room."

"I'm afraid Ed's son has different ideas from his Dad," Marla explained. "A lot has changed around here. They let Lila go the end of January and canceled the series as well. Last I heard Lila was sending out resumes looking for a full time job. Meanwhile she was getting by on unemployment insurance and a few free lance photography assignments she'd had for a couple of graphic companies."

"Oh no," Kitty moaned. "She showed such promise, and I really hoped she could replace me here." Then suddenly anger flared. "Damn it all! How could they do that—after the sacrifice I made staying here those last six months, being separated from Phil, pushing myself to establish something that both Ed and I thought would build circulation. I really cared. Besides, I thought that seeing those articles in print might boost my reputation, give me an edge when I went to look for work out West. How could they do that to me!"

"There now," Al soothed. "I know it isn't fair, but that's the breaks, Kitty. We've had a few unwelcome surprises to adjust to."

Kitty turned to Marla. "What about my replacement? Or did he eliminate that whole segment of the magazine?"

Marla rolled her eyes in response. "Wait 'til you meet her. Best you judge for yourself."

"Now Marla," Al interposed. "Give the kid a chance."

Good, old softy Al, Kitty thought. What a sweetheart he is. Always kind, willing to extend a helping hand. But now she was curious. "What's her name? Sam ... something? Is that what I read in the staff index? How about introducing me. Is she in this morning?"

"Let's go see," Marla suggested. "It's been great fun seeing you, but it's time I got back to work, and you, too, Al. Remember deadline is four 4 p.m. today, and you know what that means these days." And she rose to leave as Al reluctantly lifted himself from his chair, and with another hug of farewell for Kitty, sent her and Marla on their way.

"Samantha, there's someone here I'd like you to meet," Marla spoke as they approached a surprisingly young, little twit of a girl, who looked to be no older than Julie if she was that old. Astonished, Kitty understood immediately why Marla had rolled her eyes when she'd asked about her replacement. Without offering to rise or extending a hand of greeting, the figure before them swiveled in her chair as she reluctantly turned from the computer where she was focused. "Oh, Marla, it's you," a petulant voice responded, obviously annoyed at having been interrupted.

"Samantha, I'd like for you to meet Kitty Lundstrom. As you know she is the one who started the Home section for the magazine—your predecessor until a few months ago."

"Mrs. Lundstrom," the girl stiffly responded, still not rising from her chair or showing any sign of recognition or interest. Kitty offered the usual expected remarks of greeting even as she marveled at what she was seeing before her. It was not only the age of this person that surprised her but ... what had Ed been thinking when he hired someone so young? Or was it his son who had made the selection? She stared in disbelief at this strange being. How in the world could she possibly have the background and experience to explore home and family issues? And what would the magazine clients think if they caught a glimpse of this creature with her spiked, dyed, black hair, deadly pale complexion, dark burgundy lipstick and numerous piercings? The three little earrings on each lobe weren't bad, but as Kitty looked at the silver nose ring she couldn't help wondering who let this one out. Not to mention the full-blown rose tattoo that bloomed from the low-cut neckline of the tee shirt tightly skimmed over her breasts

"I'm sure you two will have things you'd like to talk about," Marla continued, as she slid a chair across the floor to indicate Kitty should stay for a visit. "Sorry, but I have to run. Stop and say goodbye before you leave, Kitty," and Kitty found herself left alone with her alien replacement.

That devil. Marla did this deliberately, Kitty thought, as she tried to regain enough composure to address this Samantha person. "Are you enjoying your new job?" she asked.

"Yes, and no," the young girl boldly admitted. "I like the work all right, and they're paying me pretty well for a starter position, but there are so many changes I'd like to make to the character of this magazine, particularly to my section.

The stories you were presenting may have been right for you to do, but I'm hoping to make some big changes, and Mike apparently likes my ideas." Kitty couldn't help but notice the familiar way she referred to the boss as Mike. Everyone else had more respectfully referred to him as Mr. Harper. "Seems to me the publication is old and dowdy—needs to be brought up to date. You know, made more upbeat, something that will appeal to the current generation, focus on more urban lifestyles and environment. All that overdone, country-cluttered home stuff seems dated. You know what I mean? That housewifey, cutesy stuff most womens' magazines put out. I'm no Martha Stewart. I'm more interested in metropolitan life. Give me downtown condos, brick lofts, hardwood, and steel. That's the sort of thing I want to feature. What about you? What do you think?"

Overwhelmed, taken aback, by this thoughtless, tactless outburst of criticism for all Kitty thought she'd accomplished in establishing the *Family Matters* section overwhelmed her, and she hesitated before replying. Had the readership they wanted to attract to the magazine changed, or was it just this young upstart? Then trying to be honest, yet tactful, she replied, "Well that certainly is a different approach from what I strove to present."

"I know," Samantha continued, "and what you put out may have been just right for my grandmother and you, but that was a different time. Don't you think its time for something more "with-it"? The world can't go on living in the past forever."

A different time. Kitty smiled at the irony of it. After all, it was four whole months since she'd vacated that desk. Then, annoyed by the turn of this whole conversation, she promptly excused herself and got up to leave.

Steaming, indignant, she needed someone with whom she could vent her reactions before she blew a gasket. Unfortunately, Marla was not at her desk, so there was no outlet there, no one with whom she could share observations of this outspoken creature from outer space she had just encountered. All she had to go on was the way Marla had rolled her eyes when she first asked about her replacement. What is the world coming to, she mused as she hurried from the building.

# Chapter 19

*I*t had been a disturbing visit. Out on the street, even the beautiful spring day couldn't dispel the feeling of irritability and annoyance that meeting her replacement had brought. The nerve of that snip of a girl. Who did she think she was—the way she dared to take over and immediately try to upset the image Ed, she and the rest of the crew had worked so hard to establish. As for that son of Ed's ... and the knowing way Samantha had dared refer to him as "Mike." Did he really agree with her and plan to change the publication so completely? Ed better get back soon if he wanted to retain the character he'd planned for the magazine.

That youngster was not long on tact and certainly gained no points with me. The more she thought about it, the more Kitty fumed, and there it was. Too old! Too old to comprehend the present generation's interests. Damn it all! Ever since she'd been back home it seemed people kept making remarks, implying she was out of date, out of the loop, out of step with today's social norms, already growing moss on her back from all that Oregon rain. Am I? Sure, I set high standards for myself and others, but does that make me wrong and out of date? Do I really need to change my thinking?

Change! There's that word again. Well, if change is what they want, change is what they'll get. I'll show them I'm no antique, not yet. And I have been trying to adapt. All that bicycle riding. I'll never be a real athlete, but at least I'm trying, and I'll keep on pedaling that darned bike. And next time I go shopping, instead of looking at all the sale racks for the classic designs I usually buy, maybe I'll try some of those new tight-fitting tops and pants that Julie thinks I look okay in.

Standing on the street corner waiting for the light to turn, she glanced in the nearest shop window, hoping to catch a reassuring glimpse of herself. Was she really so dated as this young thing and Julie implied? But instead of her own reflection, the window display caught her eye. *This week's special,* a sign read. *Let Mr. Shirley give you a complete new look in just three hours.*

Mr. Shirley's. The high-fashion beauty salon in town. I wonder what he could do for me?

Kitty looked at her watch. 10:15. She didn't have to meet the girls for lunch until 1:30. If change is what's needed, why not start right now? To heck with the budget I'm supposed to be on. I need a lift, so why not start here? And without further consideration, she marched into the salon and up to the receptionist's desk. "That ad in the window. What does it cost for that special three hour makeover?"

"That would be $300," the receptionist responded. "Would you like to sign up for an appointment?"

"By any chance is there someone who can take me right now? I'm only going to be in town today," Kitty boldly responded.

"What a coincidence. This rarely occurs, but it happens Mr. Shirley, himself, just had a client call in and cancel her appointment. He could take you right now if that would work for you. I'll go tell him you're here if you like."

"Perfect," Kitty replied. "Take me quick before I come to my senses and change my mind," and she smiled to herself at the audacity of her decision.

Client, she mused. Even that is a change. When did the word customer go out of use? Seems like no one has customers anymore, even the plumber I called last Thanksgiving put on airs and referred to me as his client. Well, with what he charged for his services, perhaps it was supposed to make me feel better to be called a "client" instead of identifying me as a lowly customer, she reflected.

"You can go on in now. Mr. Shirley has agreed to take you."

As she entered his workstation, Mr. Shirley held out the limp fingers of a soft, immaculately manicured hand for her to touch. "It's nice to meet you, Mrs. Lundstrom. I'm Mr. Shirley. I understand you're wanting the complete makeover?" Mr. Shirley thoughtfully stroked his chin with one of those long, manicured fingers as he studied Kitty's appearance. "What did you have in mind, Dear? Anything in particular?"

"Frankly, I haven't given this much thought. I simply want a change, something to give me a new, more "with it" look. They tell me I haven't been keeping up with the times. What do you think?" She seated herself in Mr. Shirley's cushioned salon chair.

"Well," Mr. Shirley began to run his fingers through Kitty's hair. "For starters, you really have lovely hair, plenty of body, yet soft. But perhaps you could use a dash of color to liven it up. And a new cut. Something upswept on the side to lift the lines of your face and attract the focus to those lovely eyes of yours. A little violet shadow with a touch of brown and some darker mascara would truly make them shine. Would you like to look at some pictures or do you want to leave it to me to decide what would be best for you? Or for an extra fifty dollars, we can provide our new computer imaging program."

"Computer imaging?" Kitty asked. "What is that?"

"Oh, it's so exciting," Mr. Shirley gushed. "First we take your picture and bring it up on the screen over there. Then we start picturing changes—different hair styles, various colors of makeup, so you can try on options and get an idea of what you could look like. Would you like to try that?"

Kitty looked at her watch. "I have a luncheon date at 1:30, so perhaps we shouldn't take time for that today." Besides this adventure was already costing three hundred dollars she didn't have, she reminded herself. Best to rein in a bit.

"Perhaps I'd better just turn myself over and trust you to conjure up a beautiful, new me—challenge though that may be."

"Oh, no challenge at all. You have lovely features, you know. But if that's what you want, let's get started." and Mr. Shirley reached for the exotic, leopard-print cape the salon featured and slipped it around Kitty's neck to cover her plain, classic suit.

"Now, what do you say we start by washing your hair and highlighting it with some deep mahogany tints to accent that lovely, natural brown of yours. As for styling, I can tell more about that after I see how your hair lays following a fresh shampoo." He turned the faucet and daintily tested the water temperature with those carefully manicured fingers, tipped her chair back and went to work.

Three hours later, Kitty emerged. Is this really me? My God, what have I done, she asked as she studied herself in the full-length mirror to which Mr. Shirley led her? A stranger looked back—even though she knew it was the same middle-age woman. Only now she had dark reddish brown hair, streaked with tips of a deep purplish color. On the left side of her face, the hair was clipped short except for one long front lock that swept across her forehead to hang shoulder-length along the right side of her face. A new silver clip— an extra fifteen dollars— held these strands back to permit a glimpse of shadowed violet eyes. Who was he kidding? Only Elizabeth Taylor has violet eyes, she thought. But the mascara he used did seem to lengthen her stubby eyelashes. It's extreme, but no doubt about it, he's given you a new look just like you asked for, she reminded herself. Perhaps I should have come here before going to the magazine office. That way I could have competed with my replacement for the spot of number one weirdo on the staff. One thing is all right, however. I rather like the lipstick he's chosen and the cream he massaged into my skin left it feeling velvety soft and smooth.

Then, suddenly she thought of Phil. What would he

think? He'd always loved her long, light brown hair. Well, too late now. Smoothing the wrinkles from her same old conservatively tailored skirt and jacket, she prepared to leave. She swallowed hard as she handed the receptionist her credit card. Was she supposed to add a tip to that three hundred-dollar special price for Mr. Shirley? It was his shop. Wasn't the rule to tip the employees, but not the shop owner? Or was that out of date, too?

Taking one more questioning look in the shop's full-length mirror, Kitty shuddered. What had she done? Was this really her? She'd always gotten by all right before, but... And I could swear they've done something to that mirror to help flatter their "clients," she muttered to herself. It makes me appear slimmer, and I know that's simply impossible after three hours of sitting in that god-awful makeover chair. If this is style, forget it! Who was Mr. Shirley trying to kid?

Suddenly she was furious. Makeover? Makeover my eye— freak show was more like it. Turning to the receptionist she burst out, "You call this a "beauty" treatment! I might better have gone to the dog groomers. At least they throw in a free pedicure."

The two customers who sat quietly awaiting their own appointments turned to stare, then anxiously turned away as if to ask, is that what's in store for me? By now, the one long lock of purple tinted, dark, red-brown hair Mr. Shirley had swooped across Kitty's forehead had drooped and started to cover her face. Irritably she brushed it from her eyes, snatched her credit card from the receptionist's waiting hand, signed the slip, and slamming the salon door behind her flounced out.

As she walked down the street to the restaurant, she studied herself in every shop window and felt sure half the people she met stared at her in amazement. She was late arriving at the restaurant, but it still took at least fifteen minutes before she got up the nerve to enter and meet her old friends. Old friends? Same old friends, but who was she?

"Kitty, is that you?" Janie gasped, as Meg and Paula

swiveled in their chairs for a better look.

"I'm not Kitty anymore. Call me Cat," Kitty shot back, then softening a bit she slid into the empty chair waiting for her at the table. "Sorry. I may look different, but I'm afraid it's still me." Kitty forced herself to smile as she self-consciously studied the expressions on her friend's faces. Her lower lip quivered, as Janie leaned over to offer a reassuring hug. Tears welled in Kitty's eyes, threatening to smear the lashes of her "beautiful violet eyes."

"It's not bad—just a surprise, that's all," Janie comforted. "What's happened?"

Forcing herself to smile at her own foolishness, Kitty proceeded to tell of her morning adventures—the little twit of a girl who had so infuriated her, and how she'd decided to prove her wrong. She mimicked Mr. Shirley as she revealed detail after detail of her experience at the salon, all the while mocking her own stupidity and laughing with the others at the picture she painted. "Oh my God," she groaned. "What have I done? As shocked as you all are, what do you suppose will happen when Phil gets a look at me—not to mention Madge?"

Again, Janie placed a comforting hand on Kitty's arm. "It'll be all right." she reassured her, as Meg in an effort to change the subject, interjected.

"It's just as well the restaurant isn't crowded at this hour. Otherwise, with all our laughter they might throw us out. What do you say we order a bottle of champagne to celebrate the new "Cat" in our midst? I'll signal the waiter."

\* \* \* \*

Over the years these four had seen each other through numerous difficulties, always with reassuring understanding. Theirs was a friendship always to be counted on. When Kitty had been depressed at the thought of moving, these were the women who offered to help her sort and pack, helped with the garage sale, saw that she didn't get lonely during those weeks and months after Phil left while she was still waiting to move. They'd been there for Paula during that awful year when she and Jerry finally decided to call it quits and he married Carolyn. And how pleased and excited they all had been for Janie, when after years of trying, she unexpectedly found herself pregnant at a time when the rest of them were struggling to survive the difficult teen years with their kids. Would she ever have such friends again, Kitty wondered.

The waiter arrived to take their order. "How about it, champagne, white or red wine? I'll spring for a bottle on this occasion." Meg swept her eyes around the table. "Champagne okay?" And the foursome nodded agreement as they settled down to ordering the rest of the lunch. "Place the wine on my ticket, please. Otherwise, individual checks," Meg added, as she asked for the chicken, avocado and citrus salad.

Gradually the conversation resumed, and as had occurred so many times in the past week, Kitty found herself speaking about the move, her new home, the change of climate and her life in Oregon. Then the focus turned on Paula, as Meg teased, "Isn't it about time you filled Kitty in on your new love life?"

Paula blushed a little as she chided Meg, "Oh, you and your big mouth. Never could keep a secret, could you. Besides, I'd hardly call it a love life. After all I've only been out with the guy three times."

"Three times!" Janie exclaimed. "Sounds like you've got a live one this time. Something serious here? Everybody else that's come along you've rejected after one cup of coffee. Tell us more. Who is it, how did you meet him? Come on, tell all," she commanded. And for the rest of the afternoon as they chatted and ate, Kitty and her problems seemed forgotten. But as they separated, to each go her own way, Janie pulled Kitty aside. "Something tells me, there's more to this makeover of yours than a mere encounter with your replacement. What is it Kitty? Any way I can help?" she offered.

"Not really," Kitty replied. "I'm afraid I just have to do this for myself—have to figure out who I am, and who I want to be. Perhaps it's a menopausal thing—time to admit I'm no longer the sweet, demure young thing I used to be."

"Kitty, that's not true. We all are getting older, but really, you'll always be you. And I for one wouldn't want that ever to change. I have to run now, but remember, I'll always be here for you if you ever feel like talking." And giving Kitty a squeeze of farewell she turned to return to the office, as Kitty headed for the parking garage where she'd left her car that morning. That morning. What a day this had been.

* * * *

Kitty could hear the 5 o'clock news coming from the television as she let herself into Madge's house. How would Madge react to her new image? Reluctantly, she stepped into the living room where she found Madge dozing in her favorite recliner. Apparently she'd had a long, tiring day at the hospital. Not wanting to disturb her rest, she was turning to go to the bedroom, when a sleepy voice asked, "Kitty, is that you?"

Who else could it be Kitty thought as she turned back and cautiously responded, "I think so."

More alert now, Madge raised the back of the recliner. "What do you mean you think..." then as she caught a closer look at Kitty she exclaimed, "What happened? What have you done to yourself?"

Chagrined, hesitant to admit to what she now saw as total foolishness, Kitty blurted out, "I decided it was time for a change—and look what happened." Again tears threatened as she went on to recite a sequence of the day's events. The more she elaborated, the more ridiculous she felt.

Struggling to repress a smile, Madge soothed, "Oh, Honey. I knew you were feeling confused and vulnerable, but I must say I never expected this. Come on. Seat yourself in a chair and let's talk. By any chance could you use a little mothering from your old friend?"

Close to tears, Kitty nodded her head affirmatively, as she replied, " I sure need something. I just don't understand why life seems so upside-down right now. And at the moment I feel utterly stupid. Do I look as ridiculous as I feel?"

"Well, I must say, that high-style hairdo definitely isn't the same old you. Why don't you go in the bathroom and freshen up a bit, get out of those high heel shoes if you like, and I'll go fix us a drink to relax over while we talk. Which will it be at the moment, tea, wine, or something stronger?"

"Perhaps I'd better have some tea. I already had a couple of glasses of champagne with my friends, and whatever my appearance, I still intend for us to dine out tonight, " Kitty replied. "Unless you're ashamed to be seen with me," she added as she rose heading for her room.

\* \* \* \*

Waiting for water to boil for the tea, Madge contemplated the situation, searching for words of comfort and wisdom she might offer. Why is she having such a difficult time? Does she need a therapist? Surely not, she's a bright creative woman who can find the answers on her own. When she left here I suggested she keep a journal to encourage her to take a good look at herself and analyze the opportunities and possibilities the future might hold as she enters her new life. Why does it bother her so that she's turning fifty? Why, no one even thinks of that as middle-age anymore. Middle-age! How ridiculous that seems today. Just think of all the exciting things that have occurred for me in these past eighteen years since I turned fifty, and I still feel I'm in the middle of my life. There's so much more to come.

The kettle started to boil, and she reached for the tea bags and teapot. I'll make a little party out of this, use my fancy cups. Maybe that will cheer her up, she decided, as she arranged a tray to carry to the other room. But what in the world could they do with that haircut?

"Kitty, what's really bothering you?" Madge asked as she set the tea tray on the coffee table. "What's all this talk of having to change? What's wrong with the same old you? Just because you've moved to a new location doesn't mean you have to change your whole being along with your address. What you are experiencing is simply a transition. Have you been keeping a journal as I suggested?"

"I have to admit I haven't touched it. First it was a matter of getting the new house in order. Then I became involved with the fun of decorating and—guess I just never got around to it."

"No need to apologize, but I do wish you'd try it. Seems to me you've been keeping a lot of disturbing emotions bottled up inside. Perhaps it would help if you'd open up a bit, try putting some of those feelings into words where you can look at them. Doing this might help you better know and understand yourself. I do this sometimes and it helps me chart a path to move on. Just a thought. But let's talk more about that later. Enjoy your tea now. Forget about today's foolishness. I'll call Mary, my hairdresser early tomorrow morning and see if she can come up with an idea for a simpler, less high-fashion cut. Maybe she can even do away with those purple streaks. Meanwhile, drink up, and lets go enjoy that lobster dinner you promised. Remember they have those high booths there. If you're concerned about your looks, we'll just hide in a corner.

# Chapter 20

*L*ong after going to bed Madge lay there, the conversation she and Kitty had shared over dinner kept echoing through her mind. This inability to adjust to change was so unexpected, so unlike Kitty, the friend and neighbor she had known. That crazy stunt she pulled today—that ridiculous makeover—whatever had gotten into her? She was always such a cautious, practical soul when it came to making decisions. Whatever drove her to such a disastrously, impulsive action now? What is it that's really bothering her?

Is it just that she's afraid to try something new? Surely she's not that set in her ways. And the fact that she's about to turn fifty can't be that upsetting. But then young people today do seem to make a big deal out of turning fifty—or thirty—or sixty for that matter. Sixty five I can understand. That's when Medicare and all those benefits of senior living kick in. But fifty? For most women, life, their own life, is just beginning at fifty. Up to then they've either been somebody's child, wife, or mother, and though it seems that kids today take a lot longer to grow up and leave home, surely with the upbringing Julie and Johnny have had, they are basically able to look after themselves. This should be Kitty and Phil's time to focus on their own lives for a change.

Madge remembered what an awakening that stage of life had been for her. Not only were the kids gone from home, but then her husband also decided to leave her. Such a shock. At least Kitty still has a good husband and marriage to see her through. So why is she finding it so difficult to get on with life?

Seems to me she fusses too much—like worrying about Julie calling her old-fashioned. Well, she is, in a lot of ways. But basically, there's nothing wrong with that so long as she respects and is tolerant of other's views. It did surprise me a little the way she was so shocked when I observed that perhaps it was just as well for kids to have a chance to explore living together before marriage. Like it or not, such appears to be the norm today, and she might as well get used to it if she expects to maintain family harmony.

Madge turned to her side and once again fluffed the pillow under her head. But still her concern for her friend continued to nag as another thought came to mind. Sometimes Kitty seems to blame her upbringing for making her the person she is today. But what good does that do? It's her fault if she chooses to stay that way. The words of a poem she'd encountered when trying to reconcile the changes that came into her own life came to mind.

She'd read the lines of that poem, taken them as a challenge—a dare to accept and confront reality and move on to make a new life for herself.

Those words helped me grow—helped me become a stronger, more independent person, she now acknowledged. They led me to where I am today. And where will this life takes me in the future? A satisfied smile crossed her face as thoughts of Paul came to mind. Whoever would have thought, that at my age, someone like him would come into my life. I'll see if I can locate a copy of that poem for Kitty to read. Maybe it will inspire her as it did me.

With that she switched on the lamp by her bed, opened the drawer of the nightstand where she kept paper and pencil for moments like this and began brainstorming, searching for ideas that might help Kitty find a new direction for her life. One by one she jotted down her thoughts, sometimes crossing them off as quickly as they came. Finally, a new idea came to mind, one she didn't immediately reject. Kitty had always talked of how someday she wanted to write a novel. Why not now? Madge's mind raced ahead. She could build the story around a young woman about her own age. As she creates a story of that character's life and analyzes the events and influences that make her the person she is trying to portray, perhaps it will lead her to review and analyze her own life.

Someplace she'd read that when we look at our past, we transform the present. Would doing so help Kitty understand and resolve the uncertainties she is presently going through—help her become the person she'd like to be "when she grows up"? Perhaps it's an idea worth mentioning anyway. I do wish she would get back to writing. She really does display talent. The articles she wrote for *Maine Scene* are proof of that, and Madge turned off the light and waited for sleep to follow.

* * * *

"My last day here," Kitty murmured as she slipped into robe and slippers and walked to the kitchen. The smell of coffee and sounds of Madge already bustling about unloading the dishwasher made it clear she was the sleepyhead again this morning.

"Good, you're up," Madge greeted. "How about some breakfast? I have some fresh bagels and cream cheese, or would you prefer eggs this morning?"

"Bagels sound good. I haven't had any of those since leaving the East Coast. They were never a favorite of Phil's."

"Bagels it will be, then. By the way, I called the beauty shop, and Mary's agreed to work you in during her lunch hour, unless you've decided to hang on to that high style hair-do. By the way did it survive the night or was it one of those one-night stand affairs?

Kitty laughed. "Well, I did the best I could with it this morning, but I'm delighted you have an "in" with Mary. Let's just hope she can do something for me." She poured herself a cup of coffee and refilled Madge's mug as her hostess set the rest of the breakfast items on the table.

As they began to eat, Madge broached the thoughts she'd

had after retiring the night before. "How about it, Kitty? Would you like to hear my ideas? Or do you prefer to work things out on your own?"

"It certainly can't hurt to hear your thoughts. I've always admired your ability to think things through and come up with words of wisdom," Kitty responded.

Madge rose and went to her bedroom, returning with the sheet of paper she had scribbled on in the night, plus a copy of the poem she kept to serve as a reminder to continue her own outreach for life. "You realize, Kitty, that in the year or so before I moved into this house, I'd been through a period of trial and transition in my own life. I, too, confronted unexpected change. Admittedly, to my way of thinking there's a big difference between going through a divorce and moving across the country. Divorce is an earthquake that shatters and breaks. A move is a mere tremor. It may shake things up a bit, but the foundation and walls are still there.

"Oh, Madge. I'd no idea what you were going through. You never let on,"

"I know. I tried so hard to hide my feelings at that time. I don't know. I suppose I was embarrassed, ashamed. You were a stranger to me then. But when Charlie announced he wanted out, my whole life fell apart. I felt totally lost, like a bridge floating in mid-air, disconnected at both ends. I was alone with no one, and nothing to cling to. I had so much to learn. I even resorted to counseling, but your situation is different. I'm not at all sure you need that. With Phil's help, I think you're quite capable of working things through on your own. Here, read this poem. I ran across it back when I was trying to find myself after the divorce. It made me think. It challenged me ... no, dared me, forced me to accept what was and reach out for a new beginning. See what you think." Madge handed the verse to Kitty, then rose from the table to get the coffeepot and refill their cups, while Kitty read

## Resisting Change

How well I learned the lessons of my youth,
taught by parental lesson and example,
of patience, thrift, controlled expenditure
of emotion, health and wealth.

Those lessons plague me now, though
years and circumstance have changed
my point of view.
Where is the spontaneity I seek
supporting new beliefs in
saying Yes to life?

Remote controlled, I cautiously
weigh the pros and cons of
each invitation to adventure —
of purchases for needs or pleasure —
still guided by those same parental principles
of patience, thrift, controlled expenditure
of emotion, health and wealth.

Anonymous

"Hmm..." Kitty laid the poem on the table. "It does make one take a good look at herself, doesn't it. We may not all be tied to the same old lessons, but our childhood does have a way of staging us for the rest of life."

"And not just our childhood," Madge interjected. "All the little experiences we encounter as we go through life make us who we are today while the future lies ahead like a blank book waiting to be written. One thing that helped me Kitty, was that the counselor I saw got me to start journaling. She encouraged me to write about whatever thoughts and feelings came into my mind, to get them out in the open where I could really look at them. There was so much I'd been hiding. Things I was reluctant to admit even to myself.

Sometimes we need to look back, understand where we have been in order to chart a course for where we want to go."

"Is that why you gave me that lovely blank book when I moved?" Kitty asked. "Did it show so plainly, how disappointed, uncertain I was about this move?"

"Well, you weren't exactly bubbling over with enthusiasm about the situation," Madge reminded her.

"And I'm still not sure how I feel about it. I was so attached to my life here. But it was more than that. In those last months before Phil decided to take the new job, he'd become so withdrawn and depressed. I guess I never appreciated all that he was going through at the time. I was so excited about my own new life and my job. Sometimes I wondered if Phil was just jealous. Then I began to wonder if all the dissatisfaction he was feeling and his complaints about the college were just in his imagination. Were all his concerns warranted or was he just being paranoid? Maybe he was losing it, losing his drive, his ability to come up with fresh ideas? And when I'm honest, I sometimes still worry about his ability to handle this new job. He's all on his own and has so much responsibility. It's not always easy to be a self starter."

"Have you talked with Phil about this?"

"Talk? I hardly see him. He's been so busy. Besides I can't just blurt out all these worries and doubts. It might destroy him. Right now he seems to have found a new vitality, a new self-confidence. Besides, you know how men are. They never like to talk about personal things, feelings and such."

"I know, but I've always thought of Phil as being different from a lot of men. Just like he let you decide whether or not you wanted to take the job at Maine Scene when you were wavering about the impact it would have on the twins. Unlike a lot of husbands he didn't try to tell you what to do. He left it for you to make your own decision."

"That's true. And I sometimes resented that. After all, the decision I was making was something that would impact the whole family. Why shouldn't they have a say in my decision?

I don't know, maybe it was just my own uncertainty. Maybe conflict with the values I adopted while I was growing up and my reluctance to take full responsibility. Tell me Madge. Am I just wishy-washy? Too willing to let Phil make decisions for me?"

"I can't answer that, Kitty. What works for you might not work for me. Still … I don't mean to intrude on your privacy, but I must admit I've often wondered … as upset as you were about the move, did you ever consider leaving Phil? Refuse to go along with his switch?"

"Oh, Madge, you know I couldn't do that. Why, that idea never entered my mind. I love, Phil, and besides holding the family together has always been my top priority."

"Some women would have, you know," Madge replied.

"But not I," Kitty was adamant, didn't hesitate for a moment as she responded. "That's contrary to my whole value system, old-fashioned though that may sound. I know how destructive divorce can be. Look how it messed up my early life. I never could forgive Mother for what she did. I missed Daddy so much after he left. Grandma and Gramps were good to me, but it was different living with them, different from what other kids my age were going through. No, I would never leave Phil."

"Never is a very strong word, Kitty. You're always so sure of what you believe. Is there no room for compromise? "

"What are you suggesting? Is there something I don't know about Phil?

"Oh no. Don't get me wrong. I'm not suggesting anything of the sort. Just trying to make you think. I don't really believe in divorce, either, but from experience I've come to believe there are times when it's the best solution for everyone. When a marriage reaches the point where people are just living together, taking each other and life for granted, or turning sour inside, I tend to think that can be more destructive than divorce. It may seem deadly at the time, but sometimes the separation frees everyone to move on, and rebuild new lives."

"Perhaps you're right. Certainly that's one area where childhood experience cemented my beliefs," Kitty acknowledged. "I think I'm beginning to understand why you feel self reflection is so important. Perhaps a personal journal exploring my beliefs would help. I'm afraid I've always thought of keeping a journal as being like a diary. I tried keeping one of those once when I was about eleven or twelve years old, approaching adolescence and discovering boys. I ran across that souvenir when I was packing to move. I swear every entry read something like, *It snowed today. Went to Laura's after school. We hid in her room and talked about Max and Leon. I think Max likes me.* Something stupid."

Madge laughed as she rose and went for the coffeepot preparing to refill their cups. Intent on analyzing the thoughts she wanted to express, Kitty simply covered her cup with her hand as she continued, "But I see what you mean about now recording deeper thoughts. Goodness!" Kitty glanced up at the clock that hung above the sink. "Have you noticed what time it is? If we're going to get to Mary's in time for her to tackle this hair of mine, we'd better get a move on. No more coffee or chitchat for either of us. But promise me we'll continue this conversation when we return. Already you've helped me open my eyes. I'm afraid I've just been letting myself drift, refusing to seriously put down new roots ever since I moved—even as I found pleasure in prettying up our new home." And with that she pushed her chair away from the breakfast table, carried her dishes to the sink and prepared to leave for the beauty shop.

## Chapter 21

Returning from the beauty parlor, Madge turned the key in the door and held it open for Kitty to enter. She stopped to check the mailbox then followed into the entrance hall where she found Kitty, standing before the mirror, evaluating the new short-short hairdo Mary had managed. "Reminds me of the buzz-cut Johnny decided to try when he was ten," Kitty remarked. "Oh, well, it's better than it was."

Madge stroked her hand over the top of Kitty's head. "Soft as a kitten," she remarked.

"Guess that goes with my name, anyway." Kitty laughed. "But I feel more like a new-shorn lamb, one of Mary's little flock. But I must admit, I rather like what she's done—at least she's managed something less extreme, something more in keeping with my personality. And it certainly will be easy to care for—wash and wear, no need even to use a blow dryer."

"It will grow," Madge encouraged, "and really it's quite becoming. Makes you look young and carefree."

"But what will Phil say when he sees me like this?" Kitty groaned. "Suppose he'll ever let me leave home alone again?"

"Don't worry about that now. Just remind him you're both starting a new life. Speaking of which, where were we when we rushed off to Mary's? You said you wanted to finish that conversation. What do you say we go find an easy chair in the other room. Could you use another cup of coffee while we talk?"

"Thanks for offering, but no thanks. Another swallow and I might float away." Kitty smiled as she kicked off her shoes and curled up in a corner of the sofa.

Madge assumed her usual spot, seated in her comfortable recliner. "Now, where were we?" she asked. "As I recall we were talking about how our past influences the present and the importance of self reflection. Something about how unless we question, come to understand where our ideas, beliefs, values, whatever you choose to call them, come from we often fail to acknowledge the impact these have on our present lives. The point is, it's through self-reflection we start to grow."

"Hmm... Is that what Julie was trying to say when she accused me of holding old-fashioned ideas?" Kitty questioned.

"Only you or she can answer that. I wasn't there, didn't hear what she said, only your interpretation of the conversation. But speaking of growth, I've been thinking about the way changes occur as we grow, and last night while I was pondering your plight, an interesting metaphor came to mind. You know how I've always been a plant person." Madge turned in her chair as she pointed to the bay window in the adjacent dining room. "I know you've never had the interest in houseplants that I have, but have you noticed the new plant I've started over there? Over there," she repeated as she pointed specifically to a simple green plastic pot placed next to the collection of African Violets, Begonias and Orchids she kept on display in what she called her green-thumb corner. "Go take a look at that one. See how it's just beginning to sprout?"

Uncurling from her nest on the sofa, Kitty padded over in her stocking feet to take a closer look. "This one with just those three little stems sticking up?" she asked. "They look like the alfalfa sprouts I sometimes put in salads."

"That's the one. Remember a long time ago, I think it was while Johnny was in cub scouts, he started work on some sort of merit badge. Anyway, he brought me a packet of tiny seeds he'd been given so I could plant some and watch them grow just as he was doing. I don't remember how Johnny's project turned out, but not long ago I ran across the last of those seeds. I'd put them away and forgotten about them. Just for fun, I decided to plant a few and see if they would still grow. And behold. After all those years they've taken a hold."

"So I see," Kitty nodded.

"And in a week or two, with a little nurturing, those sprouts will begin to leaf out, spread, and each shoot will develop branches. Those branches will grow, fill out and develop leaves, and as the leaves green up the plant will, in time, start to bud."

"That is if one has a green thumb like your." Kitty teased. "If it were my plant, I'd probably forget to water it and all those little shoots would curl up and die."

"Don't go putting yourself down," Madge scolded. "Besides we're really talking about people here, for people are like plants, you know. You've always been a people person and while I spent time nurturing plants you were busy nurturing your family. The nurturing you gave helped them develop into the strong young adults they're becoming today. And while you were tending to them, just like the packet of seeds I set aside for a number of years, you set aside other parts of yourself, your interest in writing, for instance. When I planted those old seeds, I was afraid they might have shriveled and died, but look at them now."

"I think I see where you're going," Kitty interjected. "Those years of rearing my family were just one stage of my growth and development. My focus at the time was on my family, but now I'm entering a new stage. Am I right?"

"You've got it," Madge acknowledged, then continued with her analogy. "The point is that like those plants, even as you were focused on your family, you were still growing, leafing out, to put it in plant terminology. Early on, you had great dreams of what you wanted to do, what you wanted to accomplish with the education you'd received in college. Then you decided to put that dream aside, just like I did with Johnny's packet of seeds. You stayed home to care for your family, and that was a very satisfying time for you. You really leafed out and grew through that experience. But as the kids grew up and became less dependent on you, you began to feel a need for something more to fill your life. I remember how you told me then that you wanted to get back to writing, wondered if you still had the talent and ability for it."

"Oh, yes. I remember how unsure of myself I was then, but I remembered the words one of my professors wrote on the last story I turned in while I was in his class. *You have a talent which may easily escape unless you keep at work on your writing.* I was so inspired by his recognition. I had the best of intentions and even started a novel. But then the twins came along, and..." Kitty left her sentence hanging in midair.

"And how do you feel about that talent now?" Madge prodded.

"I don't know." Kitty hesitated.

"Well, what's stopping you from finding out? What is there to keep you from reaching out and testing your ability again? I wasn't sure those forgotten seeds would sprout, but I potted them anyway. You'll never know unless you try, Kitty, and what better time than now to see what develops."

Kitty was obviously weighing this possibility in her mind as Madge continued. "As I recall, Phil always dreamed of doing something to preserve the natural world. He lectured, instilled his ideas in other minds, but until now, what chance did he have to actually put his theories into practice? Could this be the real reason he decided to make the move to Oregon? Was he seeing it as an opportunity to actually make a difference? It must have taken a lot of courage to make that leap, to decide to risk, to take a chance, to reach for a vision he'd held for all those years? So, how about you?"

Ignoring Madge's final question, Kitty angrily shot back, "Well, if that is what was on his mind, why didn't he just come out and say so?"

"Whoa, Kitty. I'm only guessing, asking if it's a possibility.

But with the way you just responded, I wonder—could it be he hesitated, fearing you'd think him ridiculous, that the very idea was impractical, too big a risk?"

"Well, why wouldn't I? He had a good job here; he was tenured, our life was secure, and who knows what may happen now?"

"I understand, Kitty. Changes are never easy. We all like to have a safety net, but is safety more important than aiming to fulfill our dreams? I don't know, but in your situation, at least for the present you still have the economic safety net. It isn't as if Phil had run off in some mid-life crisis looking for a sweet young thing to dangle on his wrist while he drove a red convertible. He made sure you'd still have an income and would be able to help the kids through college. Didn't you tell me Phil encouraged you not to take a job unless you wanted to? Seems to me he's offering you the opportunity to take a chance, just as he has, to reach out for whatever it is you really want. So why not use this stage of life to try to fulfill your dream?"

"But it's so impractical at my age to think a book of mine might ever get published. Do you know how hard it is to get a publisher to even look at a manuscript these days?"

"No, but I do know you'll never find out unless you try. Besides, what does age have to do with it? Are you old enough to remember the book, *And Ladies of the Club*? As I recall, the woman who wrote that was way up in her eighties when it was accepted for publication, and it was her first book. What's more, it became a best seller, as I recall. The point is, she was older, but she also had a lot of life experience from which to write that made her story authentic. You wrote well when you were young, Kitty. But just think how much you've experienced in the last twenty years to enrich and lend credence to what you have to say."

Kitty was quiet, obviously considering Madge's comments, then she remarked, "I did consider trying to do some free lance writing before I took the job at the magazine, but then that offer came along, and it seemed so much more practical to take it. I knew it would be interesting, and I was sure I could do what was required. Besides, there would be an assured salary, and at the time we were having to watch our pennies pretty close with the kid's college fees coming up. Phil knew I'd always wanted to try my hand at a novel, but... Do you suppose that's why he always referred to my position at the magazine as "just a job"—always treated it as though it wasn't a real priority—not the center of my life like his career was for him?"

"I couldn't say about that. It always seemed to me Phil was pretty cooperative about your going to work. Not like a lot of husbands who refuse to pick up some of the extra load at home."

Lost in her own thoughts, Kitty ignored Madge's comment. "I really did like my job there. I took it seriously. It seems strange now, but look how I wouldn't even ask for time to go to Oregon when Phil said he'd found a house. Andrea couldn't believe it when I told her I'd felt the commitment I'd made to the magazine was more important. That really was kind of weird, wasn't it? What do you suppose made me do that?"

"I'm not sure, Kitty. Perhaps you really hadn't accepted the idea of moving. Perhaps it was just because from early childhood you'd learned to seriously accept responsibility and dedicate yourself to completing whatever you started. You were always so conscientious about whatever you took on."

"You're right about that. Even Andrea commented on how I always let work take precedence over fun and pleasure. She tells me I was an overachiever. Said my life lacked balance. That I needed to take more time to play."

"Is that why you suddenly developed such an interest in bicycling?"

"In part, I guess. That and the fact I could see middle-age spread creeping up around my middle."

Madge laughed. "Middle age. Have you ever given any serious thought to that term? What is middle age anyway?

How long do most people live today? Getting back to the plant analogy I was making. I think of people who are in their fifties as being comparable to plants just emerging into that final burst of greening up before they finally start to bud. And that's where I'd say you are right now, Kitty, experiencing that last big spurt of growth before maturing and bursting into bloom. It's yet to be seen what sort of flower you may turn out to be, just like those seeds I started over there. But now is your time to care for yourself. You've passed from adolescence, through early adulthood, and now the buds of maturity are forming. You're entering a new stage of life. You say you've been feeling lost, don't know who you are, or what you want to be. That's not abnormal, Kitty. Your roots have been disturbed. Transplanting shocks both plants and humans. But with a little tender care, plants survive. And so will you. Your roots are still strong and firm, ready to take on new growth—new adventures."

"And a new way of looking at life," Kitty added.

"That, too," Madge's voice displayed a new, vibrant tone of urgency as she realized Kitty was understanding and had started to look to the future instead of the past. "Don't be afraid to tackle your novel, Honey. And who knows where it may lead. Some day you may turn out to be a Pulitzer prize-winning novelist. On the other hand..." she winked as her eyes twinkled and a knowing smile lit up her face, "should Julie or Johnny marry, you may find that the real peak experience of your life comes with being a doting grandmother. Don't forget that most plants bloom more than once, and you still have many years and many opportunities in which to blossom. The point is not to be afraid to reach out, reach deep inside and search for your true self. That's the real challenge and it's something no one else can do for you."

Madge sat back, quietly waiting for a response from her friend. Had she said too much, spoken too freely? Finally, a soft quiet voice responded. Kitty rose from the sofa, walked across the room and stooped to place a kiss on

Madge's cheek.

"Oh, Madge. How lucky I am to have you. I'll have to sleep on all this, think it through, but already I can begin to see where this may lead." Enveloping her friend in a warm daughterly hug she whispered "I love you." Then as she released her, she added, "But for now I'm afraid I must bring this visit to an end. It's time for me to pack my bag and get ready to leave for home. But don't forget. You know I'm expecting you to come to Oregon this summer. We can continue this conversation then, and who knows? Perhaps I'll even have a start on a new book by then." Quietly she picked up the shoes she had slipped off and headed for the bedroom where she would spend the last night of her first return visit, to the town where she used to live.

## Chapter 22

Cruising along the interstate headed home, Kitty relived in her mind all she'd experienced during this, her first trip back home. "Only it isn't home anymore," she murmured. This unexpected acknowledgement came as a shock. But she knew it was true. Oregon was where she belonged at this time of her life. Madge had insisted from the time Phil first announced he'd taken a new job there, that the move represented a new opportunity for both Phil and her—a chance to reach out for adventure. A time to let her own life bloom, as she now explained it.

What a selfish ninny I've been, she now scolded herself ... feeling sorry for myself, crying about what I was giving up, always looking back instead of ahead. Adventure? I think I'm finally beginning to understand what Madge has meant all along. To Madge, adventure and change were one and the same. Yes, it was time for a change, time for her to challenge herself and try something new, just as it was for Phil.

Could it be Madge was right about the real reason Phil decided to accept the job in Corvallis? Somewhere she'd read where men are more concerned with a wider, broader view of the world while women focus more closely on home and family. Was this just a stereotypical view or a true general characteristic? Perhaps Phil did see this new assignment as an opportunity to actually do something important to save the environment. She'd have to talk with him about that. If this was true it would help her better understand what he was going through. If only he'd visited with her more about his real motivation instead of just complaining about his dissatisfaction with where he was. Men! Why can't they ever talk about their real feelings?

Her thoughts drifted off as she thought of Phil. She missed him, wished he was here with her right now. She had so much she wanted to tell him. First, she wanted to thank him for suggesting she make this trip. She'd discovered so much these past few days.

Why, only now am I recognizing the extent to which I tried to keep our lives tied to the past and our old, comfortable rut. The way, even after I moved, I continued to cling to the past—even when planning and organizing our new home. Even then I kept planning, thinking of it as a place the four of us would share, refused to accept the fact that the twins are already building their own new and independent lives. But after seeing them this weekend... Johnny seems so mature, and Julie... yes, seriously involved emotionally this time. Why couldn't I understand, accept that before?

Yes, Phil was right. This was the right time for us to move on, to reach out for this new opportunity to build a rewarding future.

* * * *

It was a lovely spring day, and the sun blazing on the windshield made the car seem stuffy and warm. Too early to resort to air conditioning, she decided, and she pressed the automatic button and cracked open the front windows. A stiff breeze ruffled her new short-short hair-do. Not yet accustomed to the chill of the draft that whipped across her neck, she flipped up her jacket collar for protection. This new hairstyle was going to take some getting used to, but at least Mary had been able to restyle Mr. Shirley's dreadful cut so she looked like a human being again. In fact, now that she was getting used to it, she quite liked her new look. It did make her feel young and carefree. The color was still too red, but at least the purple streaks were gone. Thank goodness Madge had an "in" with her operator. It was yet to be seen what Phil would have to say about his new Kitten.

Kitten? There was that name again. If she was really

going to change, to become a mature person, shouldn't her name also change? Was that why she'd already introduced herself to Christine as Kate? Why not? There'd never be a better opportunity—new community, new setting, new lifestyle, a new person, a new name, a new career. It won't be easy, I know, but I am going to take a chance, try my hand as a writer for awhile. Another gift for which I have to thank Phil. How lucky I am to have such a thoughtful, kind and loving husband. Only now did she appreciate how carefully he'd planned this move—miserable though he may have been in his old job he hadn't run off half-cocked. He'd waited until the right fit came along—a position with enough income to provide the safety net on which they'd come to depend. This wasn't some wild mid-life fling as she had secretly feared

Once again, Kitty's thoughts drifted back as she replayed in her mind all that had transpired during the past week. The image of that little twerp who now held her old job came to mind. Still annoyed by the incident, she couldn't help thinking how much that girl had yet to learn—her greening up, leafing out period of life, as Madge referred to it, still lay ahead for her. Samantha. Somehow that name didn't seem to fit the person she'd met any more than Kitty belonged to the new person she sensed herself to be. Samantha—a sweet old-fashioned name, one far too sweet for such a little snip. She needed something more pseudo-sophisticated, saleable, brisk, to portray the person she'd met. Sam perhaps? Something smart and uni-sex to keep her clientele guessing—something short, snappy, stylishly modern—all glass and steel like she claimed to prefer. Shame on you, she scolded herself. Now you're being downright nasty, catty. Forget about her.

Foolish to carry on so about that incident, but the more she replayed their encounter, the more she realized how perfect the timing of her leaving the job at *Maine Scene* had been. She'd left at a time when she could still feel good about the publication and the work she was doing. She'd hate to be back there now, just putting up with the situation as Marla and Al seemed to be doing. Poor Ed. She worried about him, wondered how he was getting along. But maybe it was time for him, too, to adjust to a new time and a new stage of life.

What fun it had been to lunch with old friends, good reliable, understanding Janie. And what about Paula? It would be wonderful if she'd actually found Mr. Right. She'd made the best of it following her divorce, but it was obvious she was lonely. How her eyes sparkled when Meg teased, but just as with Madge, a new radiance shone through at the prospect of finding someone new in her life, someone for whom she cared and one who cared about her

Then there was Julie. Had she been overly protective, offered unwanted advice too freely in her determination to make Julie see things her way instead of allowing her to discover these truths on her own? Probably Phil and Madge were right. Maybe she did need to loosen up, adjust to the present, but... It would be hard to release the apron strings, quit trying to protect her children. As their mother she knew she would always be concerned for them. But was she really being overly protective? Was she really too hide-bound, too entrenched in beliefs and teachings she'd clung to all her life to accept the reality of the changing mores of today? And what was it that Madge had said about her one day being a doting grandmother? It would take awhile to get used to that idea. Once again her thoughts wandered. A grandmother? How could that be, she wasn't old enough, not yet, but someday. She allowed her mind to roam, conjuring images of once again holding a tiny baby in her arms, watching a toddler—a little girl all pink and white—running toward her with open arms. "Not yet." She spoke aloud as she forced herself back to the reality of the present.

She thought about the journal Madge had encouraged her to keep. If she weren't driving, all these rambling thoughts going through her mind just now could be written there, refined perhaps, maybe be used later in a book she would write. I'll dig out the draft I started before I took the job at *Maine Scene*, see if it has possibilities, and it occurred to her the story she had started then was still with her, stored away in her mind. Over the years it had often come to her and new thoughts, new ideas briefly focused to enrich or expand its content.

The more she thought about a book prospect the more her imagination soared. Her fingers itched to get back to her computer. Even if writing is a solitary, sometimes lonely profession, it's something I enjoy, she thought, and the opportunity to work part time for Christine would provide relief from the long hours I'd have to spend alone. And silently, she vowed, I'll follow through as soon as I get home and explore that contact with a group of other writers like my new neighbor suggested a month or so ago. Why have I put that off until now, she chided herself.

And then it came to her. Home? I not only said it, I meant it. Home, our home in Oregon. I'm beginning to grow up. I'm reaching towards maturity. I'm finally ready for this new stage of life, ready to move on, ready for a new life, in a new house, a new town with new opportunities. Change? Why not? Not my hair, not my figure, but a new approach to work and play—a new way of thinking for a new stage of life. And a new name! What better opportunity to lay that baby name to rest. I'll always be Kitty to Phil, to old friends and acquaintances, but now... "Call me Katherine, Katherine with a K." She spoke aloud, testing the sound, testing how it would feel to grow into her true name.

Reach out. Let yourself dream Madge had advised, and dream she would. In her mind's eye she visualized the novel she would write—the author's name Katherine Bremley Lundquist boldly printed across the cover—a grown-up name for a grown up, mature young woman.

The exit sign at the edge of the road caught her eye, and off to the right she saw evidence of food and lodging. A sudden pang of hunger swept through her. She glanced at the clock on the dash. Already it was nearly five. She'd left Madge's place a little after noon. Time to pull off and take a break, find a stop for her first night on the road and get a good early start tomorrow. Best not to wait too late in the evening to look for a room. She had no reservation. Excited with all the possibilities the future held, she could hardly wait to call Phil and tell him of her plans—let him know how much she appreciated his suggesting she make this trip back to their old home. And they would talk like they had when they were young and full of dreams. Once again she would open herself to share her inner being, confide the private thoughts, the uncertainties troubling her which she'd been trying to keep hidden. She and Phil would deal with these things together. Only in this way could they regain the innocent trust, the unity of being one she had known when they were younger— before life interfered and they drifted apart, each in his own way. For that was what she had allowed to happen.

Yes, she had grown, was wiser for all that had happened these past few days. It had been wonderful to go back to visit, but it's looking forward that matters now, she realized. And with this thought firmly planted in mind, she pulled into the exit lane and left the freeway.

# Chapter 23

*It's 10:30 p.m., but I'm too excited to sleep. It was wonderful talking with Phil earlier this evening. For the first time in months we really talked. I miss him so—can hardly wait to get home, to be with him again. I told him all about the conversation I had with Madge, the plans I've made, and the promises I'm making to myself to see them through. Like my decision to start journaling. And even though I don't have that beautiful blank book Madge gave me here to write in, I'm starting now. The fact this is written on motel stationery will serve as just one more memory of this tremendous day—the first night in the new life of Katherine Bremley Lundquist. I must remember to tell Phil about that name change, but I hope he will continue to let me be his "Kitten." I like the intimacy of that private name used only by him.*

*It's hard to know where or how to begin when starting this journal, so I've decided to think of it as writing a letter to myself. That way I can chatter on about whatever comes to mind. I've learned a lot about myself these past few days— my past, present and future. I've already become more introspective. It seems that in the past I felt I had always to keep busy—needed always to be doing something, taking care of needs outside myself, so I rarely took*

*time to really consider what was going on inside.
Pragmatism is the word that comes to mind. But if
I'm to become a writer, and this is my ambition now,
I will need time for inner communication. Only then,
as I learn to internalize thoughts and feelings, will I
be able to understand the character and motivations
of others.*

*I've so much to be grateful for, for Phil, especially.
How fortunate I am to have such a loving, patient
and understanding husband. And Julie, Johnny,
Madge. What a true friend she is. Would I ever have
reached this stage of development if she hadn't come
into my life all those years ago? But it's getting late.
Time to set aside these pages and go to sleep. But I'll
be back. 'Night now.*

## About the Author

As a wife and mother of three sons, Meyer spent much of her life living and working as a home economist and teacher in rural central Idaho and Eastern WA.

Now retired, she resides in Spokane, WA where she enjoys the opportunity to pursue a long-held interest in writing. She is the author of two previously published books: *Peaceful Valley, The Story of Kamiah's Early Years*—a historical memoir telling of her grandparents and the part they played in founding the village of Kamiah in NezPerce Indian territory. A second book, *Uphill Both Ways,* is an amusing travel memoir recounting the challenges and triumphs encountered as a novice rider bicycling 100 miles in the Catskill Mountains.

*Call Me Katherine* is the author's first fictional work.

Breinigsville, PA USA
29 November 2009
228340BV00001B/5/P